THE FENNISTER AFFAIR

Sally was beginning to feel that there was something dark and sinister about all that happened on this ship, about most of the passengers, certainly about the officers.

How was it that Dr. McRae arrived before she had time to return from the bridge? Dick could have been on watch and chanced upon her and Tim. But weren't they out of sight at deck level? But perhaps not from the bridge? Then had Captain Crowthorne seen Tim and sent at once for the doctor, the sailors, even Dick?

She looked up at him. A hard look, he noticed, nothing hysterical about it.

"He was deliberately poisoned," she said slowly, "because he knows things some people want kept hidden."

THE FENNISTER AFFAIR

JOSEPHINE BELL

day books

A Division of STEIN AND DAY / *Publishers* / New York

FIRST DAY BOOKS EDITION 1981
First published in the United States of America in hardcover by
STEIN AND DAY/*Publishers* in 1977
Copyright © 1969 by Doris Ball
All rights reserved
Printed in the United States of America
Stein and Day/*Publishers*/Scarborough House,
Briarcliff Manor, N.Y. 10510
Library of Congress No. 77-21305
ISBN 0-8128-7056-5

CHAPTER I

Sally went on board the cruise ship *Selena* in mid-after-noon. Her uncle took her to the quayside in his car, grumbling a little at having to miss half of his siesta, but conscientiously performing his duty to his sister in England. He had promised to look after Sally in the two months during which she would work for him as secretary, checking references, checking the index, making a fair copy, or rather three copies, of his new book on the remaining small parts of the British Empire. *Residual Empire* he was calling the book. He had begun it six years before he was appointed to his present job in Bermuda. Several chapters had been lost to independence in other places before Bermuda provided enough leisure to overcome this discouragement. Several more chapters had been lopped away since. But the work was finished now and Sally, preserved in health and spirits, or so he believed, was leaving the island that afternoon.

She was not going straight home. His gratitude was real enough for generosity. Also the winter cruise season was drawing to an end with March passing into April. It had not been difficult to secure a cabin for his niece on *Selena*, that old favourite, for the Caribbean part of the trip and, if she chose, for the return voyage from Bermuda to England.

"You can let me know how you like it," he said, mopping his face with a large silk handkerchief when they had climbed the gangway to B deck and stood under the shelter of A deck above. "If you'd rather fly out when you get back here again, just let me know. Otherwise I'll confirm that you keep your berth all the way back."

"Will they be able to keep me?"

"Shouldn't wonder." He glanced about to see that no porter or loiterer was in earshot. "*Selena* often carries immigrants, not so many now as formerly, of course, but it's cheaper than by air. Only they're so superstitious, you understand—"

"You mean the poor woman who disappeared?"

"Presumed lost overboard," said her uncle, slowly. "Bit of a mystery. Hope the passengers won't bore you with it. Not their business but you know what people are."

"Isn't it—I mean, wasn't it—their business? Wasn't she with her husband? Poor thing, he must—"

"He left the ship, I understand and is to stay here in Bermuda until the legal side is settled."

"Legal? I don't understand—"

The Chief Steward, a tall figure in tropical white uniform, came up to them with a sheaf of papers joined to a board.

"Miss Combes? Miss—Sarah—Combes?"

"That's right."

She smiled, glad to have the sad conversation interrupted.

"We understand my niece's cabin has been changed," her uncle said. "From a single on C deck to a double, now vacated, on B deck. That's where we are now, isn't it?"

"Yes, sir. If you will follow me I'll show you where to go."

He led them to a door, pushed it open, told them automatically to mind the step and pointed along a narrow lighted corridor.

"Number Ten, Miss Combes. You will find your luggage there. Tea will be served in the passengers' lounge, which is on A deck at the after end. Stairs *that* way inside, or outside near the swimming pool."

Without waiting for any answer the Chief Steward disappeared again. He had learned from long experience that passengers found their way about best if left to themselves. It was no good explaining the geography of the ship to them. Some picked it up quickly, others stayed uncertain right through the voyage. But they had nothing else to do except eat and drink, sleep and amuse themselves. So let them find their own way around. *Selena* was a small ship as passenger ships go. He had only sixty bods to look after this trip.

"Will you have tea on board?" Sally asked her uncle a few minutes later. They had found the cabin, very roomy for one, they had both exclaimed. The suitcases had arrived and had been put one on each of the two luggage racks.

"I'm clearly expected to be a couple," Sally said, laughing. "I wonder which is the best bed to take?"

Her uncle was looking at his watch.

"I won't stop for tea," he said. "Your aunt expects me back. Besides, you'd better start to get to know the people on board."

"Won't they have gone ashore sightseeing and shopping?"

"Maybe. Yes, I suppose so. At least—"

They had both remembered the bereaved husband of the lost woman. Sally thought, with renewed pity, how ghastly it would be to go ashore alone, away from the monster that had swallowed up his companion, never to know how or where or when. A mystery, they'd called it. She almost wished she had decided to fly home.

In silence they reached the head of the gangway.

"Don't let this thing depress you," her uncle said rather helplessly. She smiled at him for his understanding.

"I won't. It isn't as if we knew them. Give my love to Aunt Hilda and thank you both more than I can ever say for my time here and for giving me this cruise."

She had planned what she wanted to say but now found she could not finish it. So she hugged her uncle and they kissed on both cheeks and he told her what a

7

help she had been. Then he clattered away down to the quay, looking far too hot, she thought. She watched him go back into the Customs shed and then turned away. The outside stairs, she remembered, beside the swimming pool; that sounded promising.

But the passengers' lounge was quite empty, a large, bright, cool emptiness, air conditioning and fans humming, small tables everywhere with small chairs set beside them, large chairs lining the walls. But not a soul beside herself, not even a steward.

There had been very few new passengers waiting to embark, she remembered. In fact only the eager-faced young man who seemed to be an experienced traveller from the way he handled his luggage and produced documents before they were asked for.

She looked at her watch, comparing it with the clock on the wall of the lounge. Then sat down in one of the chairs against the wall. There was a bell quite near her, marked Steward. No doubt someone would come if she pressed it. So why didn't she? Because her uncle had refused her shy invitation to be her guest? Because she was alone and unwilling to seem to be eager for her tea? Because she now realised that if she had come up to A deck by the inside corridor and stairs she would almost certainly have met a steward in the extension of the lounge on the other side of those glass doors she was now facing?

Along which a figure was moving towards her, an elderly female figure in a pale lilac-coloured dress, using a thin black stick to help her slow steps.

Sally watched a slim white-uniformed male figure overtake the lilac one just as the latter reached the glass doors. He held them open for her and followed her into the main lounge. Tea, Sally thought, wondering if she ought to stand up; company, too. She moved a little forward in her chair.

The lilac woman did not seem to have noticed her. She moved towards a table where the waiter was already placing a cup and saucer in position.

"Yes, tea please." She turned her head as she sat down, raising her voice to ask, "Won't you join me?"

Sally was beside her in a moment.

"Tea for two. China with lemon for me and for Miss—?"

"Combes," said Sally. "Sarah Combes. Sally. I'd like China as well, only with milk."

"Thank you, madam. Thank you, miss," the steward said, hurrying away.

"My name is Fairbrother," the older woman said. "Agnes Fairbrother. I think you have only just come aboard and that your—escort—has now gone back ashore."

"Yes," Sally agreed. "How did you know all that?"

Mrs Fairbrother laughed.

"I had just got up from my siesta," she said, "when you came up the gangway. I was sitting further along the deck here, in the shade. I saw you both at the foot of the gangway. Later I saw him—"

"My uncle," Sally said. She explained what she had been doing in Bermuda and what she was now to enjoy.

"Lucky girl," said Mrs Fairbrother. "So many of your age seem to take their holidays so hard. If they aren't actually working for their transport and their keep they are pounding along in jeeps or caravans."

"Or bicycling or pony trekking," Sally laughed. "Or sailing. Only I love that. I've been doing some here."

Their steward came in again with a tray. Another one followed him with a trolley of sandwiches, bread and butter and cakes.

"We have first choice today," Mrs Fairbrother explained. She glanced at the clock. "But the others will be back very soon now. Passengers have to board again by five. We sail at half-past."

"Yes, I know," Sally said, relieved. "I was told we left at five thirty. I've been wondering where everyone had got to."

9

"Oh, they'll be back," Mrs Fairbrother said. "I think they may have been making the most of the break."

She paused, looking gravely at Sally.

"I'm sure you will have heard of our—tragedy," she said in an altered voice.

The girl nodded, waiting to hear more.

"You will have had the news in your papers and broadcasts, of course," Mrs Fairbrother went on.

"Just the bare fact. I mean—"

"There *was* only the bare fact." Mrs Fairbrother spoke calmly but her eyes were watching Sally with great attention. "The Fennisters were at dinner as usual. At the Captain's table, where I sit too. The next morning, that is today, two hours before we berthed, we were told that Mrs Fennister had disappeared from the ship and must be presumed lost overboard."

"How appalling!" Though it had been in the Stop Press Sally had not realised the accident was so recent. "When was she missed?"

"A good question," Mrs Fairbrother answered. "Mr Fennister went to bed early for him, apparently. That is to say, before midnight. He woke up in the early hours and she wasn't in the cabin. He went to find her— No result."

"There wouldn't be anything anyone could do," Sally said. "My uncle said Mr Fennister had gone ashore."

"He couldn't go on with the cruise, could he?" Mrs Fairbrother suggested gently.

"No. No, of course not. What a frightful way for it to end."

"The cruise or the marriage?" asked Mrs Fairbrother.

Sally was repelled. She found the question cold-blooded. Finishing her tea in silence she got up to go. Mrs Fairbrother was reaching for the teapot to pour herself another cup but already voices in the other part of the lounge told of new arrivals. The passengers must be returning.

"Will you excuse me?" Sally said. "I think I ought to

unpack before we move. I think I'm a pretty good sailor, but—"

"But you never know," Mrs Fairbrother said, with a smile and a wave to a couple of newcomers who were approaching her table. "And last night it was very rough. Run along, Sally. I'll see you again after dinner, if you're still about."

This time Sally went through the glass doors. There was a bar at the far end and several card tables along the side nearer the open deck. Again a generous array of chairs. The bar steward was in place behind his counter and beckoned to her as she approached.

"Excuse me, miss, but may I have your name, please? For settling up your account."

"My account?"

"For drinks and such, miss. Tea comes on the all-in."

"Oh. Oh yes, I see."

She gave her name and even remembered the number of her cabin.

"That would be on B deck, miss, wouldn't it?"

"Yes, that's right."

The man gave her a queer look but said no more. She went down the wide inside stairs from A deck, noticing that on the starboard side of the ship, the opposite position to the bar lounge which was on the port side, there was a reading and writing room with the ship's library on shelves behind glass fronts.

Though she had told Mrs Fairbrother that she intended to unpack before the ship sailed she felt, on reaching her cabin, all the restlessness and suppressed excitement of departure. She had met a number of people in the passages, carrying parcels, laughing and talking, comparing the hotels and restaurants where they had eaten during their brief hours on shore. There was much shouting too from the quay to the ship and a clanking of chains and bars.

So she abandoned the boring task she had proposed and went out on deck, noticing as she did so that the gangway had already been drawn in and the heavy warps that held the ship to the bollards on the quay were being loosened.

Very few of the passengers were interested in *Selena*'s movements. But a young man who had a suitcase at his feet, a haversack on his back and an elaborate camera hanging round his neck was standing not far from the door that Sally had left. It was the man she had seen before, who appeared to be so efficient, so knowing. She went up to him.

"Did you just make it on board or have you just missed leaving?" she asked him, smiling broadly.

The young man, who had glanced round as she reached him, smiled back.

"Just made it," he said. "Narrow shave. Ought to have decided earlier."

"Decided what?"

"To come."

They looked at one another, coolly appraising, neither embarrassed, each very much accustomed to ordinary exchanges with total strangers. But the conversation died there. The look went deeper than the words and in each case reached a barrier. Sally's was natural to her. She was always friendly but never very forthcoming. She knew that her looks pleased men, so she made no advances, prepared to wait and discover by being discovered. Besides, he was lying. She had seen him go through the formalities for embarkation ahead of her. He must have decided a couple of hours ago.

The young man's attitude, on the other hand, was professional, since as a journalist his curiosity was limitless, but impersonal, at least at the start of any fresh acquaintanceship. So now he removed his gaze from the very attractive face beside him, picked up his suitcase and, murmuring something about finding the purser, pushed himself and his luggage through the door behind him.

Sally continued to watch the ship's movements as the vessel took herself away from the closely lined quay in a series of skilful movements. It was not until *Selena* made her final turn and moved out to sea that Sally realised the whole thing had been done with the help of tugs, that now stood away from her with final shouted orders and cries of farewell. Turning away from the deck Sally went back to her cabin, regretting that her impulse to speak to someone of her own age had prevented her watching an interesting manoeuvre.

She unpacked slowly, thankful that the ship's movement was hardly noticeable. Aunt Hilda had suggested that the passengers would certainly change for dinner, so the girl, after a quick shower, put on a dress she had worn at her uncle's house when people came in for drinks informally. She was determined not to overdo the conventions, but she had never thought it amusing to defy them just for the hell of it.

She found herself seated for dinner at the Captain's table beside the new young man. The Captain would not be dining until later, the steward said.

Mrs Fairbrother, inevitably, Sally thought, was sitting on the other side of the young man. She nodded to Sally and began at once to introduce her to the rest of the table.

"Mrs Longford. Sir John Meadows. Lady Meadows. Miss O'Shea. Miss Combes. My name is Fairbrother. And yours is? . . ."

"Tim Rogers," said the new young man, nodding vigorously to each of the others in turn except Sally.

"Mr Rogers. So now we all know each other," said Mrs Fairbrother, sitting back with a sigh of relief as the steward began handing round plates of fresh melon.

In spite of Mrs Fairbrother's social lead there was very little conversation at the Captain's table that evening. Mrs Longford made some effort to be kind to Sally, but the Meadowses and the rather severe-looking Miss O'Shea scarcely said a word, either to one another or to the newcomers. They ate steadily through the three course dinner, then excused themselves and left. Mrs Longford stayed for a cup of coffee, then rose herself.

"They are still upset, you see," said Mrs Fairbrother gently. "You must forgive them. It was only yesterday it happened. Last night—in the night—perhaps this morning very early. They sat at this table. Actually in the places you two are now occupying."

"Good God!" Tim said. He had already gained a fair picture and account of the accident, if that was the right way to describe the disappearance. He had looked at the facts, such as they were, from the journalist's point of view. Now he was being presented with a very strong local reaction and one that confused him.

"Of course," Sally said, in a hushed voice. "The places should have been left empty. How very tactless of the stewards. We could have been put *anywhere*."

"I don't know so much," Tim said, looking round. Though nearly everyone had now left the dining saloon the tables near the Captain's had been fully used. Anyway it was no good minding now, the meal was over.

"Let's go up on deck," he said abruptly to Sally, swivelling his chair away from the table.

But she was looking at Mrs Fairbrother, waiting for the older woman to get up and did not appear to hear him. So he muttered, "Excuse me", copying Sir John Meadows's intonation and went away, rocking a little as he reached the stairs and taking hold of the handrail as he mounted.

Sally did not see him on her way to her cabin. When she reached it she found she was not feeling very well and was glad she had not attempted to join Tim on deck.

She sat down. Will power could do wonders she told herself, but it was only reasonable to prepare for the worst. So she looked about and saw no receptacle at hand, not even the paper bag provided on aeroplanes. On the other hand there was a small contraption like an empty frame fastened to the side of one of the bunks, that looked as if it were meant to hold a bag of some sort.

This was the bed against the inside wall of the cabin, not the one under the window, where she now saw the curtains waving inwards and then collapsing outwards with the roll of the ship.

She told herself to look for the container and keep her eyes from those curtains. She decided she would sleep in the bed against the inner wall. Very slowly and carefully, for the oppression in her stomach had now mounted to her brain, she knelt beside the drawers in the dressing table, which were empty because she had unpacked into those on the side near the window bunk.

Quite empty, the top two, she found, not daring to hurry though she knew the crisis was very near. In the lowest drawer of all she found two things; a little cardboard container to fit into the frame on the bunk and, as the drawer fell out on to the floor of the cabin because she jerked it in her now very urgent need, a bent copy of a book with a crumpled piece of paper sticking out from between two pages of it.

Relieved of the whole of the excellent ship's dinner, Sally fixed the brimming container into its proper place and flopped on to the bed, weak and trembling. After a minute or two she had recovered enough to ring for the cabin stewardess. A motherly hand to put her to bed; even more important, remove her shame and equip her for its possible recurrence.

But she was disappointed. After a long interval a young man appeared to report that the stewardess on B deck was off duty and was there anything he could do. Her shame was redoubled. Obviously she was the only passenger who suffered: all the rest were sea-hardened, damn them. Her indignation sustained her until the steward had done his work and provided her with fresh equipment and a glass of water.

After he had gone away she found she was holding the book with the piece of paper still in place between two pages. The volume, she found, belonged to the ship's library. The paper was part of a letter. On it was written a message that drove away Sally's seasickness for several hours.

'I cannot bear it any longer,' the message read. 'If you love her more than me you must want to be rid of me. I won't stand in your way, my darling. I will simply disappear. Felicity.'

Which was exactly what the poor woman had done, Sally thought. Felicity. Felicity Fennister. Overboard.

Too easy, she thought, rolling over to find the new little cardboard box. At that moment she longed to follow the missing woman's example. But exhaustion overcame the wish and very soon she fell asleep.

CHAPTER II

She woke in the middle of the night, shocked to find herself still in her clothes. Her head ached, her mouth was foul, she was very thirsty. When she had drunk a little from the glass the steward had provided and had waited a little to see what would happen, she found she was distinctly better though still shaky. So she crawled off the bunk and undressed and washed and crawled back again. Before she turned off her light she put the book she had found on the dressing table and the paper with the message into her handbag.

She was roused a few hours later by a knock on her cabin door, followed before she was awake enough to answer by the appearance of a stewardess, who asked at once in a pleasant foreign voice "And how does madam find herself today?"

Without waiting for an answer the stewardess marched over to the window to pull back the curtains, fasten them, stoop to gather Sally's clothes from the floor and push in the drawer that had fallen out of the dressing table the night before. Then she stood up beside Sally's bunk and repeated her question.

"Empty," said Sally, smiling up at her.

The stewardess nodded. She was handsome in a Spanish style, dark eyes, an olive skin, abundant, rather coarse looking black hair. She wore a straight white overall, belted loosely and with short sleeves.

"How did you know I was sick last night?" Sally asked.

"The steward who attended you make a report. You are bad sailor, madam?"

"No," Sally said, indignantly, sitting up. "At least, I'm never bothered in planes. And I've been doing a fair amount of sailing in Bermuda."

"Your pills were no good?"

"I didn't bring any. I never have. I didn't think . . ."

"Without pills . . ." The stewardess shrugged her disapproval of such foolishness and then said, more kindly, "Madam will take a breakfast in bed?"

Sally nodded.

"Coffee please and toast. Would it be safe to have a boiled egg? I do feel horribly empty."

"It is always better to have something inside," the stewardess said and went away on this rather ominous note.

But all was well. Sally got up feeling perfectly fit and an hour or so later went on deck to find a chair in the shade. As she looked about her at the recumbent figures staring out to sea or reading their magazines and books she remembered the book in her cabin. She went back to find it and as she reached the cabin heard voices inside it and found the stewardess near the door talking to the steward who had answered her call the night before. The stewardess was holding the book Sally had come to fetch.

"I've just remembered it," she said, holding out her hand. The stewardess looked at her but said nothing.

"The book," Sally told her. "I found it last night. I want to take it back to the library. It belongs to the ship."

"I will take it," the stewardess said.

Sally continued to hold out her hand. The woman had obviously not understood.

"I'll take it myself," she said, "because I want to get out a book to read. So give it to me, *please!*"

The quite unusual note of command in the girl's voice had its effect, more so perhaps since the steward had finished his sweeping and stood just behind the older woman, wanting to get out of the cabin, too.

The stewardess gave the book into Sally's hand with a thrust like a blow. She nearly dropped it but managed to clutch it to her and stepping aside into the cabin allowed the two to escape, which they did in opposite directions along the corridor. Book in hand Sally went thoughtfully up to the Reading Room library.

There were several people sitting at tables writing and one or two browsing along the shelves. The Chief Steward, whom Sally recognised as the man who had guided her uncle and herself the day before, was sitting at a table near the door. He had an open book ruled in columns before him, she noticed. The records of borrowings, of course.

He greeted Sally with a welcoming smile which faded when he saw the book in her hand.

"I found this in a drawer in my cabin," she said. "It must have been left there by someone, possibly on the last cruise, otherwise—"

She opened her bag and took out the paper she had found in the book.

"Only *this* was inside it," she said. "Between two pages. I should have missed it but I upset the drawer and the book fell out and it fell out of the book. This paper, I mean. Look!"

He took the paper and read the message.

"You see," she said. "Now please can you explain? Did her husband take out the book or did she? Did she put that message in it for him to see? Did he see it?"

Her voice had risen a little as she asked these questions; several heads turned in the direction of the Chief Steward's table.

"I don't know," he said, in a very low voice.

"But you must know who took out the book. Perhaps it wasn't either of them. In any case I must send this message, this paper, to Mr Fennister in Bermuda."

"How?" asked the Chief Steward.

She held out her hand for the paper and after a rapid glance at those around, now once more preoccupied with their own affairs, he gave it back to her.

Sally dropped it into her bag again. She moved away to the shelves, found a book and took it back to have it

19

registered. The Chief Steward, writing carefully, said, "I think you would be wise to give that paper to the Purser, Miss Combes."

"Why?" she asked, still nettled by his answer, revealing but unhelpful, to her former intention.

He was not to be drawn. He gave her a polite smile and turned to the next passenger who wished to borrow a book.

Sally went down to B deck. The recumbent figures in the shade had not moved. She went along towards the swimming pool, wondering for the first time that day what had happened to Tim Rogers. Had he suffered too? Or was his stomach the cast-iron variety? Or had he knocked it out with pills?

Mrs Fairbrother called to her as she passed.

"You were not down for breakfast, my dear," she said, as Sally took an empty chair beside her.

"No. I was sick last night, so I thought it was safer to start quietly today."

"We were all wondering if you were upset at having that cabin," Mrs Fairbrother said gently.

"Because it had been the Fennisters'?" Sally asked.

Two sturdy middle-aged figures stopped their walk beside them.

"Finished the constitutional?" Mrs Fairbrother asked.

"Mile and a half," said the man, mopping his face with a large white handkerchief. His wife glanced about her. He moved away to find chairs.

"This is Miss Combes who joined us at Bermuda," Mrs Fairbrother said. "Mrs Newbuckle, my dear and—here he is—Mr Newbuckle."

"Combes?" said Mr Newbuckle, panting as he adjusted a chair for his wife. "Bermuda? Then . . ."

"Sally Combes," she said. "I expect you've met my uncle."

"Not this trip," Mr Newbuckle said. "But we've corresponded a fair amount lately."

Business, Sally decided. That prosperous stout figure,

flat Midland accent, grey eyes that were screwed up now smiling, but behind the resumed dark glasses would be cold and shrewd. Mrs Newbuckle was astonishingly fat in a flowered dress misguidedly low in front and without sleeves.

"I was asking Miss Combes—"

"Sally!"

"I was asking Sally," Mrs Fairbrother persisted, "if she was at all upset at having the Fennisters' cabin."

As Sally began to explain that she had suspected it from the time she was told her berth had been upgraded to B deck, and found this confirmed when she knew it would be a double cabin with shower, she saw the deck steward coming along the line of passengers with ice cream and the time-honoured gamble on the day's run.

As she took her ice he murmured, "The Purser would be obliged if you would see him at your convenience, miss," and passed on before she could answer.

She looked at her companions. They were all absorbed in their ices or in comparing notes about how they had fared in the daily gamble up to date. Finishing her ice at a speed that made Mrs Fairbrother shudder, she got up to go.

No one tried to stop her. They probably all think I'm going to be sick again, she thought, as she found her way to the Purser's desk.

Without any prompting the Purser said, "Captain Crowthorne would like to have a word with you, Miss Combes. Would twelve noon be convenient?"

"Why, yes," she said. "What about?"

"Twelve noon, then," the Purser said. "In my office behind here. Come to the desk. Someone will be on duty."

As she turned away, baffled by the man's manner, Sally picked up one of the news sheets provided for the passengers. It had been read many times, she saw, but was not too crumpled to spoil the print. She decided not to go back to the trio she had left. She was pretty sure her coming interview was the Chief Steward's doing. He must have reported the scrap of paper to the Purser as he had advised her to do and from there news of it had gone to the Captain. Only natural, as his ship had been the scene of what now could only be taken for suicide.

She checked that the note was still in her bag, settled down near the Purser's office and read the news of yesterday. There was nothing in it about the Fennisters, neither about Mr Fennister or his missing wife. In fact nothing whatever about Bermuda. After all, why should there be? The ship's stay there had lasted barely twelve hours.

She ran through the close-typed bulletin in a very short time and when she took it back to the Purser's desk found she had only occupied ten minutes of her waiting time. So she made her way down to the foredeck and leaned on the rail watching the flying fish scuttering away over the tops of the waves as *Selena* drove through them.

By now she had forgotten the slow persistent movement. The long deep blue waves had smooth tops; there was no white anywhere except along the ship's sides and in her wake. The horizon was a far distant circle, no other vessel in sight.

Captain Crowthorne, who had seen the girl from the bridge, noted her serious expression but was pleased by her relaxed attitude. When, a few minutes later, she came into the Purser's office he rose to greet her with an equally becoming seriousness. He motioned her to a chair and resumed his own.

"I wanted to see you, Miss Combes, because it seems you have found some document or other that may help us over this unfortunate business of Mrs Fennister."

"Yes."

Sally saw no point in argument. She opened her handbag and brought out the paper which she handed over as willingly as she had previously given it to the Chief Steward in the library.

The Captain read it. When he looked up Sally explained how she had found it.

"You know of course that you are in the Fennisters'
cabin?" he said. "I can confirm the lady's name was
Felicity. If I tell you her husband's name is Mario and
the real surname Fenestri, does that convey anything?"

"No," Sally answered. Though Captain Crowthorne's
face was serious enough there was a hint of laughter or
was it derision in his eyes that annoyed her. Why should
she be expected to know who these people were and why
they used two names?

"I'm sorry," the Captain said, sighing. "You young-
sters have different tastes these days. When I was young
I loved circuses and thought acrobats were first-rate
heroes."

Sally was too much astonished to resent the first part
of this speech. She gaped.

"The other passengers haven't told you then?"

"There hasn't been time," she answered and left it
at that, not wishing to explain her weakness of the night
before.

"It is because Mario Fenestri's act, which he performed with his wife, has been—well— His contracts in
South America, too. We could not help him, so he left
the ship. But he wanted as little publicity as possible.
You can see that, can't you?"

"Certainly I can. But this message ought to go to the
authorities in Bermuda, oughtn't it?"

"Why? He is a stranger in Bermuda. There can be no
proper inquest without a body. The chances of its being
found and brought in are very small—I should say neg-
ligible."

Sally nodded. She knew very little about such things
but she still felt that the news of this clearly intended
suicide ought to be given to someone, somewhere. If
only to the husband. Unless—

"You don't think this man, Fenestri, found the note
and pushed it into the back of the drawer himself? Not
wanting to acknowledge the suicide? Not wanting to give

23

away his—his affair? If so, I'm *sure* I ought to do something with it."

She snatched quickly at the paper Captain Crowthorne had now laid down and put it back into her bag. He sighed again. A charming girl, a very pretty girl, a well-mannered girl, but like most of her kind self-confident to the point of obstinacy. Inducing, not admiration, but fury. He was accustomed to command. He held out his hand.

"I think I am the person to do what is necessary," he said. "If you will kindly give me back that paper I will get in touch with all the people concerned when we reach Barbados."

"Can't you do it at once by radio?" Sally asked, opening her eyes wide. "I've just read your daily bulletin."

Captain Crowthorne mastered his intense desire to put her over his knee and smack her bottom hard. The mini-skirt would give little protection, he saw. Instead he got up, saying coldly, "I think you are ill-advised to keep it. I should prefer to have it in my safe. However, both the Chief Steward and the Purser and I know where it is. Possibly a fake, of course. We have not compared it with Mrs Fennister's writing—that is, if we have any."

Sally opened her bag, then shut it again. As the Captain waited silently for her to get up she did so, realising at last that he had washed his hands of her at present. It was a novel sensation: she did not always insist upon having her own way, but she did expect to argue before giving in.

Captain Crowthorne was at dinner that night but neither Sally nor Tim Rogers was at his table. They had been added to the Chief Officer's table and their places taken by a couple Sally had noticed on deck sitting quietly next to one another and taking no notice of those near them.

At her new table there were more passengers of about her own age, Sally found. The Chief Officer introduced them all to one another, Reg and Nora Ford who were going out as missionaries to Trinidad for a flight on to Haiti; non-conformist of some sort, Sally concluded vaguely; Guy and Dora Cummins, for Tobago, as teachers on an exchange scheme. And Tim.

"I missed you this morning," he said, greeting her. "But I wasn't up till late. How about you?"

"Much the same," she answered with a grimace. "But for God's sake don't talk about it now."

The missionaries looked embarrassed, the teachers laughed. "We haven't forgotten the first three days," Reg Ford told her.

"I think we all want to forget all of it," the Chief Officer said quickly. As if to point his words the weather forecast at that moment came over the intercom; a reassuring, pleasing forecast of uninterrupted sunshine, calm seas, light airs.

After dinner Tim suggested a short stroll round the deck. But Sally found it cold and being unwilling to go in to find a coat and make the effort of coming out again, she said she was tired and on reaching her cabin found this was genuinely so and immediately put herself to bed. Though she expected to sleep at once she found as her body rested her mind became more and more active. Her thoughts continued to circle about the strange fragment of a letter. For a torn off scrap as it appeared to be, it had an unnaturally lucid content. The name of the writer, the dire intention of the writer, these were plain. But the person addressed, whether loving husband or discarding lover was not named, was totally obscure. Perhaps a fake, Captain Crowthorne had said. That meant perhaps planted. Quite so. But why? And when?

It was not her business, she told herself fiercely, trying hard to put away the question and go to sleep while the going was so smoothly, so blessedly good.

In the end she did so, but not before she had got up again, taken the note from her handbag and locked it into her smaller suitcase. The handbag, after all, though it was always with her, was never locked and the contents were usually in such confusion that a mere scrap of paper, if not deliberately stolen by some trick, might simply fall out and be lost.

Feeling pleasantly conspiratorial Sally got back into bed, drew the sheet over her shoulders and slept.

CHAPTER III

But in the morning Sally had changed her mind again. She now thought her action of the night before ridiculously melodramatic. At the same time she knew the strange little note would nag at her until she found out the meaning of it.

She determined to ask Mrs Fairbrother for advice. The old lady had been her first friend on board and though she had never met her before she already felt she was a superior kind of aunt or great-aunt even, good for ready advice that you need not take but that would very likely be comforting.

Her preliminary search was unproductive. Mrs Fairbrother was nowhere to be seen on deck either in the sunny rows of chairs near the swimming pool or the shaded ones under the covered parts of the deck on either side. She went the complete round at both levels twice, then, feeling too hot in spite of her cotton jumper and very short skirt, she stepped inside on B deck and read the day's news.

All the copies were in other hands, she found. But Mrs Newbuckle, seeing her search and then stand near the open door, raised her large bulk to hold out a copy to her.

"You were looking for one of these, Miss Combes? Well, here you are, dear. Not that there's much in it. A word only about that poor man, Mr Fennister. He has no plans, it seems. But they've let out who he really was."

"Some sort of entertainer, wasn't he?" Sally said cautiously.

"Did you know that? Circus act, it appears."

"An acrobat, I think."

"Really now. Fancy you knowing. Can you tell me where you saw them? On the tele, was it? They speak of an act for the two of them. What did she do? Such a quiet little mouse of a girl. Never seemed to move. We thought she might be convalescent from an operation."

"I don't think so," Sally answered. Mrs Newbuckle had run on so long there seemed to be no point now in going back to the beginning.

"I never actually saw them," she said weakly. "Does it say what he means to do now?"

She had the news bulletin in her hand by this time and glanced down at it as she spoke.

"Nothing definite," Mrs Newbuckle told her. "Fancy you knowing who they were! None of us did, right up to the end."

She stepped out on to the deck. She wanted to find Fred and tell him. Such a queer thing. Here was this girl, three months in Bermuda, hadn't she said, knowing about Mr Fennister, only he wasn't, he was Mario—like a girl's name—Fenestri. And the pair of them circus performers.

"Fred," she said, stooping over him where he lay dozing and pushing his panama hat up off his face. "Fred, I've something ever so important to tell you!"

But Fred Newbuckle only muttered, "Leave me alone, girl, can't you," and pulled the hat down over his face again. His wife turned with her news to the neighbours in their chairs on either side.

Sir John and Lady Meadows nodded to Sally as she passed them, again looking for Mrs Fairbrother. They had not read the bulletin, they told her, because they had not yet finished the copies of the Airmail *Times* they had found waiting for them in Bermuda and hoped to spin these out until they got to Barbados where another batch would have arrived. They continued their careful slow constitutional, seldom speaking, perfectly self-contained.

The Bernsteins passed them, walking in the opposite direction.

"If Sir John wants you to play bridge tonight it is we should be obliging them," Mrs Bernstein said in a low voice.

"Have I ever had objection?" Mr Bernstein answered quietly. "It is not interesting, their bridge, but it is honest."

He smiled at her.

"Those other two you will not let me play with, there it is different?"

"They wish to play only with men," he said, not answering her question.

"But they do not—fleece—the innocent lambs of Christians and school teachers," she persisted. "For that we must give credit."

"A very little credit, my Lottie, for the lambs have not grown thick coats. They are too dedicated."

They both laughed gently. They had possessed thick coats in their own youth and then total shivering nakedness with fear of death added. But very slowly in a foreign land they had managed to become clothed again, not richly but in decent comfort. It was enough that they were warm and the old wounds covered. They hoped the missionary and teaching lambs would not have to meet the extremes of disillusionment they themselves had suffered.

"It seems strange," the missionaries were saying to Mrs Fairbrother, who had moved slowly, with two floating gauzy scarves flying from her head and shoulders, to her favourite spot near the swimming pool, "that *no* one on board knew who the Fennisters really were."

"And you know now?" the old lady asked, settling herself.

"Well, there's this rumour— I think Mrs Newbuckle started it."

"Really! That surprises me very much. I read it in the ship's little newspaper. I think you'll find it there."

At this point Sally came up to them. Nora Ford repeated her astonishment over the Fennisters. Sally repeated her limited knowledge without declaring where she got it. But the arrival of Tim Rogers provided a good deal more enlightenment.

"I'm not sure if they ever performed in England," he told them.

He had squatted on the deck beside Sally's chaise-longue, though she had moved her legs to one side to provide him with sitting room. "He is Italian by birth though his wife was English. They have done European tours and were lined up for an extensive one in the South American capitals. They were leaving the ship at Bermuda in any case."

"How did you find all that out?" Reg Ford asked. He and his wife had listened wide-eyed to Tim's recital.

"I think in the course of his profession," Mrs Fairbrother suggested gently. "You *are* a journalist, aren't you, Mr Rogers?"

"Tim," he answered smiling. "Yes, mam, I work for the newspapers."

The missionaries looked startled by this form of address as being less American, coming from an Englishman, than plain disrespectful. But Sally laughed shortly and Mrs Fairbrother looked indulgent.

"I might have guessed," Sally said. "So you're here to pick up stories about the Fennisters before the accident, are you? How they appeared to the other passengers? What exactly happened? Did your paper scoop Mr Fennister in Bermuda?"

Tim scrambled to his feet. The missionaries exchanged glances and got up also.

"The ices should be appearing soon," Mrs Fairbrother suggested. "And the gamble on the day's run. I believe it was the old man in the Yorkshire party won it yesterday."

The Fords smiled but moved away, slowly at first to get their balance and then faster as they reached the rail further forward along the ship's side.

Tim said, "I'm for a bathe before the sun goes in."

"It can't, can it?" Sally asked. She was indignant at the bare idea.

"I'm afraid it can cloud over," Mrs Fairbrother said. "There does seem to be a sort of haze arriving. And the wind is certainly stronger."

She began to wrap her scarves round her head and throat.

"Here comes the ices," said Sally, lazily. She had no particular wish to move. Besides, if they could get rid of Tim she still thought she would like to consult Mrs Fairbrother about the note. When the journalist moved away she opened her bag at once.

Mrs Fairbrother read the note, held it away from her, drew it close again.

"Genuine?" asked Sally, "or a fake? I mean, planted to deceive?"

"I couldn't possibly tell you," the old lady said. "I never saw Felicity Fennister's hand-writing."

"What shall I do with it?" Sally asked, putting it away again. "Give it to Captain Crowthorne as he wanted, or post it back to Bermuda from Barbados? And if so, who to? Mr Fennister, the port authorities, the coroner, care of my uncle?"

Mrs Fairbrother laughed.

"Perhaps just post it overboard," she said, gaily.

Sally stared at her. She was inclined to be offended. It was a serious matter, the Captain and the other ship's officers had taken it seriously. She had asked Mrs Fairbrother for serious advice and got this frivolous answer.

"I think I will bathe after all," she said stiffly. "If Tim comes back will you tell him I'm changing and won't be long."

"I'll tell him," Mrs Fairbrother said.

She watched Sally swaying up the deck until she turned with a jerk and a clutch at the door handle to disappear into the corridor. The wind had increased and the ship's roll was quite pronounced. Mrs Fairbrother watched the walking passengers drop into chairs and push these back from the rail as spray began to shoot upwards.

Behind her, screened from sight, the swimming pool splashed and gurgled. Several bathers appeared from it to wrap themselves in towelling coats and gowns. A few new ones arrived, but did not at once go into the water.

Presently Tim Rogers came back in trunks with a towel draped round his shoulders. Mrs Fairbrother gave him Sally's message.

"I wonder if she will," he said. "She's not a good sailor, is she? I mean she was laid out by a very moderate roll the night we left Bermuda. This is a bit more, if anything."

He looked over the screened rail behind Mrs Fairbrother and drew back quickly as the water, swung from side to side slapped up at him.

"Better get it over," he said, discarding his towel on the chair Sally had left.

She arrived very soon after, to throw down her towel coat also. She wore a neat blue bikini that showed the good, even result of her recent weeks of steady sunbathing. Mrs Fairbrother admired the graceful brown body, neither fat nor thin, neither bony about the hips and skimpy in the bust nor bulging above and below out of that essentially unbecoming garment, the bikini.

"Tim is in the pool," she said, smiling up at the girl.

Sally nodded, adding her dark glasses to her discarded towel. She went round the corner of the row of chairs down the three steps to the edge of the water and stood with her toes over the tiled rim preparing to dive. The water was high in the pool, she noticed vaguely, still looking for the journalist. She called his name and saw three faces turn in her direction.

Then several things happened in rapid sequence. The ship dipped to her left, the water came higher still, Tim yelled a warning, she dived. In mid-air she saw the water fall away, tried to swing her arms up and her legs down and met Tim's arms held out across her body. Her weight knocked him down and the returning wave of water covered them both.

As it retreated again Tim steadied her with both hands. She was neither frightened nor angry he saw, just utterly astonished.

"All right?" he asked. There was no need to explain his action.

"Yes. And thank you." She shook herself. It had been a nasty moment. Her own fault, too. Diving into no water— She shook herself again.

"I hope I didn't squash you," she said.

"It was a pleasure."

This was true. It was a body worth catching and holding and preserving from injury. He put his arms out to steady it again as the swimming pool dipped once more, but Sally, with water under her, dived below the arms and swam the three strokes that brought her to the side. She saw that the pool was now empty except for Tim and herself, but several of the bathers were standing round the edge of it watching them.

This embarrassed her. Did they think she would perform another silly, reckless act? She must have looked a right Charlie flopping on top of poor Tim and knocking him over. She began to feel annoyed with him for the buffoonery of the act, though it had probably saved her from breaking her neck. Or was that an exaggeration?

She swam to the corner of the pool and climbed out.

"Had enough?" Tim shouted and the watching bathers giggled.

"For today, yes," she shouted back as naturally as she could. "See you later."

"In the bar," Tim said. He had followed her immediately. He was speaking in her ear as she reached for her towel. "Six o'clock. It's a date."

"You're shivering," Mrs Fairbrother told her. "Go and

33

get dressed, my dear, and join me for a cup of tea in the lounge. We've had the best of the day, I'm afraid."

A good many of the passengers had come to this conclusion already. The bridge players who had amused Mr Bernstein and shocked his wife by their undoubted, but dubious success at the game, gathered early in the lounge bar. They could not yet order drinks but they had proposed a business meeting with two other bridge-playing colleagues.

"It's this publicity," one of the bridge players said. "I don't like it."

"None of uth doeth," said a colleague with a pronounced lisp.

"You wouldn't think the general run of passengers here would be all that interested," a third bridge player complained.

"Nothing to occupy their minds," the first told him.

The fourth man said nothing, until seeing Sally pass through the main part of the lounge in search of her tea with Mrs Fairbrother he said, "She a dick or something?"

The others laughed.

"No, I mean it. First she worries the Steward chap in the writing room. I watched her. Showed him her authority or whatever. A signed order of some sort. Next she sees the Purser to make an appointment with Crowthorne. Then she sees the skipper himself and he lets her out looking as if he'd like to wring her neck."

"So?"

Two of the others sat back in their chairs considering, but the one who had spoken last leaned forward.

"I don't know what all that was about, but it didn't concern us. That's for sure. We've never been spotted because we've never used the same ship twice and never misbehaved. Not noticeably. Not to be found out."

The others were listening carefully, nodding at short intervals.

"The girl doesn't concern us, I'll swear to that. But the

young newshound who came aboard at Bermuda is well on the sniff for anything that smells. I know the sort. Freelance, I'd say and not making out too well."

"That why he joined us? This Fennister story? Woman disappeared—overboard, most likely?"

"Why not? Bermuda won't get anything more from Fennister or Captain Crowthorne. They grilled the ship's company that day and got nothing. The passengers gave nothing."

"How d'you know?"

"We'd have been held in port there if there'd been anything for them to tell, wouldn't we?"

"May be. Yes, it looks as if Fennister could satisfy them, doesn't it?"

"That his wife was nuts and jumped into the drink?"

"What else?"

They looked at one another and shook their heads.

"Balls!" said the bridge player who had spoken first. "That girl was as sane as I am."

Forestalling the obvious retort he took a pack of cards from his pocket and shuffled it briskly. Then passed it along the table.

"Cut!" he said. It was an order.

They were still playing when Tim and Sally went up to the bar together just after six. Tim, seeing them, put a hand on Sally's elbow to guide her through into the main lounge where he put her in a chair in a corner away from the various doors and asked her what she would like to drink.

As he expected one of the junior bar stewards was already hovering for orders.

"Service," Sally murmured lazily. She had been thinking as she changed for the evening that she really ought to be grateful to Tim Rogers. He had saved her from a nasty accident and he had shown a certain eagerness in wanting to talk to her now.

She waited until they had been supplied with their drinks, then said, "I didn't thank you properly, Tim,

35

for saving me breaking my neck in the pool today
I was a bit upset at the time."

"I don't wonder."

"Not by the near accident. By making such a fool of
myself."

He gave her a long hard look. Then laughed.

"I was right," he said, complacently.

"What about?"

"You."

"How d'you mean?"

He did not answer this but after looking round at
those other passengers who had by now come into the
lounge he turned to her again and said. "You know I'm
a journalist. Right?"

"Yes. I think we've all decided that."

"You think I came aboard at Bermuda to look into the
Fennister story?"

"Didn't you?"

"Not to start with."

"Oh." She waited but as he said no more she asked
"Why did you come aboard, Tim?"

"I'm going to tell you but I want you to keep it to
yourself at present. Will you?"

"Yes. If you say so."

"That's my girl. Well, I've been in South America a
couple of years now—three actually—freelance. I left my
paper in London— No, don't ask. Take too long. A
misunderstanding— So. I wander about the capital cities.
Pick up Spanish. Pick up just enough pesetas to keep
alive. Hang around the night clubs and that."

He paused to drink and Sally waited. It was not a
very new or a very interesting story. She hoped it wasn't
leading up to an attempted touch, because she had no
money to lend and today had been quite sufficiently
embarrassing already.

"I met a dancer in one of those clubs just over a year
ago," he said. "She was drinking too much. She said her
husband was in the show business but he had left her

36

and gone to Europe. I told her to stop drinking and go after him."

"Well?"

"I didn't see her again but I heard from her friends she had taken my advice. I asked them how she had managed to scrape up the fare and they said she was working her passage. On a cruise liner."

"What was she like? To look at, I mean?" Sally asked.

"Very dark. Very Spanish looking. She could speak English pretty well. Much better than I do Spanish. That was how she managed to get a job as a—"

"Stewardess," Sally said. "She's on B deck. She came to me the morning after we left—after I'd been sick in the night. Dark like you say. Very Spanish. She must be the one."

"I saw her go on board," Tim said. "I'd just checked out of my hotel. I hadn't decided what to do next. But I saw her go on board so I fixed myself up with the local paper, told them my story and got the assignment straight off. What's your girl's name?"

"She isn't exactly a girl," Sally said. "Quite a grown up woman, I'd say. Thirty, at least."

Tim laughed.

"She'd look her age in uniform. She wasn't wearing it ashore."

"There may be more than one South American stewardess on board."

"I don't think so. I've done some homework. Her name's Conchita."

"I haven't asked her name. She hasn't found her husband, then?"

"I think she was looking for Mario Fenestri."

CHAPTER IV

On the following evening there was a dance in the lounge at which the Captain appeared together with those members of his crew who were not on watch at the time.

Captain Crowthorne took his passengers' pleasures and comfort very seriously. Earlier in the cruise he had made it his business to assess these, which naturally varied a good deal according to their age and circumstances. Not that the young were fussy these days. He remembered missionaries on a ship where he began his career at sea who complained about the playing of secular, though classical, music on Sunday. A dance on that ship would have been unthinkable. But here were young Reverend Reg Ford and his wife jiving round with the best. Only Miss O'Shea, on her way to teach the multiracial children of Tobago, was sitting out, with a severe expression on her long face that might have been disapproval or just from neglect. He made his way to her.

"Can I have the pleasure?" he asked, with duly formal politeness.

"Pardon?"

"Will you dance?"

"Oh! No, thanks. I prefer to watch."

He had done his best. He moved away again uncertain where to try next. The medical crowd were self-sufficient. The Combes girl? Might be embarrassing after their not very cordial encounter. Daren't risk another brush-off. Anyway, young Dick Groves was making that way. He felt a light touch on his arm.

"Jack! Can we dance?"

It was Mrs Longford. Ann. He frowned, then relaxed and broke into a smile. They moved out on to the floor together. She began to speak rapidly and he bent his head close to hers to listen.

Richard Groves was a cadet officer on board the *Selena*. He was working for a mate's certificate and hoped to achieve it after this voyage. It had taken him a year after he left school to decide that a life at sea was what he wanted and another two years to persuade his parents that this wasn't just another of the bright ideas he had been having for his future since he was fifteen. So, having tried his hand at various unlikely jobs and made nothing of any of them, he had signed on as an able seaman for a voyage to the Far East and had found where his real vocation lay. Not as an able seaman for ever, but in command of a ship in due course. With unusual vigour and calm he had broken down the objections at home one by one, discovered how to start his career and now at the age of twenty-four was well set upon it and likely to make up time in future.

Sally Combes had taken his eye the first time he saw her, which was at breakfast on the second morning out from Bermuda. Together with the two junior wireless officers he had marched into the dining saloon. Three young men, well-built and fresh-faced, in spotless white tropical uniform, were a pleasant sight for any eyes. Sally had turned her head when she saw others doing the same and as the group were just passing her table at the time, Dick found himself gazing into large greyish-green eyes full of laughter and admiration and very close. He blushed and smiled at the new girl, for he realised she was new on board. Sally smiled and blushed, too. He decided those eyes rated a follow-up. The dance gave him his opportunity which he took at once, not realising he had cut out a half-hearted approach by Captain Crowthorne.

Sally congratulated him upon the act.

"You've saved me from the Captain," she said as they

moved off. It was a slow old-fashioned waltz tune which Dick interpreted in a rhythmic, but unorthodox fashion and Sally followed without any difficulty.

"How come?" he asked, not really believing her. He saw across her head the strong square back of Captain Crowthorne with the thin, mauve-tipped fingers of Mrs Longford spread across his right shoulder.

Sally explained. It did not occur to her that she might be indiscreet. The young man's uniform, white shorts exchanged for black evening trousers, made him part of authority, part of the ship's government to which she submitted, so long as it remained reasonable.

"I think he was right," Dick said.

"Why?"

"I can't tell you. I just think he was."

"Naturally. He's the Captain. You're— What are you? Wireless?"

"Why do you say that?"

"Tim said you were at the wireless officers' table."

"Who's Tim?"

"A journalist. Tim Rogers. Came on at Bermuda. Like me." She added, not quite knowing why she did so, "I didn't know him before."

Dick nodded, looking round the lounge to discover Tim, whom he knew well enough by sight, though he had not heard his name before that evening. The Snooper, he had called him to himself. A journalist, was he? Snooping for sensation on the Fennister story. Making up to this—more than a snappy number—more than a dish—a—a person. Not to be left to the casual uses of a Snooper.

"Seems to have taken on one of the medical wives," he said. "Have you met them? One is an anaesthetist in her own right."

"They all sit at the M.O.'s table, don't they?" Sally said. She showed no interest whatever in Tim's doings, Dick saw with exaggerated pleasure.

When the music stopped Dick stayed beside Sally and

when the record began again they resumed their dancing. He would have been quite happy to spend the rest of the evening with her. He noticed that Captain Crowthorne was again dancing with Mrs Longford and felt justified. But swinging out of a corner and narrowly missing the other pair he heard the Captain's voice in his ear. "Circulate, Groves. Circulate." He nodded submissively.

"What did he say?" Sally asked.

Dick looked at her laughing eyes.

"You 'eard," he said, trying to laugh too.

"Let's sit down," she suggested. "Then he can't get at you."

"Oh, can't he!" Dick answered. But he steered her off the floor and they collapsed, quite glad of a rest, in two armchairs against the wall.

Near them the Yorkshire contingent, stout middle-aged, prosperous, were gathered about two tables, drinking steadily. The women's voices, hard and keen as knives, reached Sally clearly.

"There she goes again! Did you ever see the like! After the poor man from morning to night. He must have the patience of a saint!"

"Patience! He may like it for owt we know. Happen she's an old friend of his."

"Friend! That sort isn't *nobody's friend*!"

Dick leaned to Sally, his face very red.

"In actual fact Mrs Longford is a friend of the Crowthornes," he said, fiercely. "Besides, she's, I mean she *was*, Felicity Fennister's sister. So naturally he's looking after her."

Sally was astonished.

"Mrs Fennister's *sister! Dancing!* I'd have thought—"

She had no time to explain what she thought because Tim came up to them at that moment to ask her to dance. She turned to Dick, smiling.

"You'll be able to obey orders now, won't you?" she said, getting up.

41

Dick had risen too. He looked across Sally's head at Tim and was pleased to find he had a two-inch advantage of him.

"Thanks for the dance," he said, in the most casual voice he could command. "Some other time. 'Bye."

He stared round the lounge to discover a possible wallflower, found one and took the floor with her, hoping to impress Sally with the speed of her replacement.

But Sally was no longer there. Tim had danced her round until they came to the double doors that opened on to the deck. He had led her through, shutting them again behind him.

It was a night of brilliant stars. The wind that had got up early in the day and made the ship roll badly again, had died off, leaving a calm sea gently building to a wide swell and falling away from it again. The air was warm but not as hot as the crowded lounge in spite of the air conditioning there.

"We ought to have waited to swim now," Sally said, moving away from Tim to the steps down to B deck.

"Where are you going? I want to talk to you."

"Down to the pool. To see if it has stopped swinging about."

"Of course it has. Come back."

But she had gone and Tim followed her, grumbling. Having satisfied herself about the pool Sally moved to the rail and stood there until Tim joined her, when she turned to him and said, "I don't understand how anyone could fall into the sea from this ship by accident. The rail is too high and too solid."

"Except where it has an opening for getting off in port or into the lifeboats."

"Exactly."

They had been through the regulation shipwreck drill that day and had seen how securely fastened these sections were.

"I suppose a bent member of the crew might have been found to unlock one, but it's a crazy idea, really.

Timing would be impossible and anyway locking it up again—"

"You're suggesting murder now, aren't you?" Sally interrupted.

"Not an elaborate suicide. If it was that, the section would have been found open."

"Right. Actually I have already ruled out accident and suicide. If she went overboard she was put there."

"You mean—dead already?"

Sally was horrified but the idea had sense.

"Or stunned. It stands to reason. The decks of a ship are never quite deserted. Crew are on watch. The bridge is manned. But no one, it appears, saw or heard anything. Or shall we say, no one has *reported* seeing or hearing anything. If any independent member of the ship's company or the passengers had done so surely they would have raised the alarm at once."

"You'd have thought so," Sally agreed. "Not just gone on or gone to bed or whatever leaving it to Mario Fenestri, if that's his real name, to make a fuss in the morning when he discovered she had vanished."

"But," Tim persisted, "if someone had stunned her or killed her and carried her up on deck—"

"Not carry. The doors are heavy enough to open, let alone climb over the sills— Carrying someone—"

"Not easy, I agree. But possible, if you're a man with very well-developed shoulders, such as an acrobat like Mario."

"Oh!" cried Sally. "Don't go on. Possible certainly. But why? There has to be a motive."

"There is one," Tim said solemnly. "The usual one. A woman. This stewardess. I've got her name, now."

"The one that looks after my cabin? Yes, it is Conchita. The other stewardess told me. She was in my cabin this evening. Just before dinner. So it must be your Conchita."

She was remembering. Tim had said Conchita claimed Mario as her husband.

"Then is Mario really Conchita's husband?" she asked. "In which case—"

"Felicity was not, and Mario—or perhaps Conchita—has got rid of her."

Tim's face was in darkness but his voice was derisive.

"Kill his act, when it's just had an unexpectedly good European tour and the offer of a first-class tour in South America?"

"Then Conchita? In which case why is she still quietly working on the ship while Mario, without apparently denouncing her, leaves at Bermuda to settle about his future?"

She shivered violently. She had remembered Mrs Longford, happy, smiling, in the circle of Captain Crowthorne's arm, her small clawed hand on his shoulder. She remembered the Yorkshire women's jokes at their expense.

"I simply don't understand her sister," she exclaimed harshly.

"Whose sister?" Tim was genuinely bewildered this time.

"Felicity's. Mrs Longford, the Captain's friend, the ship's tart, according to some of the passengers, who was dancing tonight as if nothing in the least tragic had happened."

"I see." Tim had recovered very quickly. "You're sure?"

"Dick Groves, the cadet officer, told me," Sally said, with another memory, not chilling this time, but warm and pleasing, of rotating gently to a very compatible rhythm.

"Oh, him," said Tim, sourly. He had a feeling, a true one, that the Bridge did not approve of his presence on board and were not likely to be very helpful.

Sally began to move away towards the door into the lounge. The noise from there had not slackened. She suddenly stopped and turned away, so suddenly that she ran into Tim who was following. For the second time

44

that day his arms closed round her and held.

"I've changed my mind," she said, laughing. "I'm tired. I don't want to dance any more or talk. I'm going to bed."

"Goodnight then," he said coolly and bent his head to kiss her. But she turned her face quickly and the kiss landed on her cheek. His arms fell away.

"Goodnight, Tim," she said. "See you tomorrow." And was gone.

Tim went into the still crowded lounge, made his way slowly across it to the bar and ordered himself a large whisky. The Bermuda newspaper was paying.

"Seems like that guy got the brush-off," remarked one of the bridge players to his circle. They were not playing cards now, though they had been doing so in the quiet of the writing room earlier on.

"I wouldn't say his interest was the girl, more the cabin she's in," one of the others suggested.

"There won't be anything there to help his story," the youngest of them said, with finality.

"Why d'you say that?"

"From watching Mario. Not one to leave a loose end, I think."

"Only a very big question-mark."

They all laughed gently, which made Tim Rogers look round at them to be met by four pairs of wary eyes and four faces rapidly falling into stillness.

It was not an encouraging sight, Tim found. Where most of the passengers ignored his presence or linked him with Sally, which he preferred, these men resented him. Why? Because he was a journalist? Then why again? He did not credit them with any fine feelings about a lack of taste in his coming aboard to work up a story about the drowning of a young woman in show business. Oh, no. If they resented him as much as they seemed to, it was because he might know or discover something they reckoned to hide. Such as? He gave that up for the moment. But perhaps Felicity Fennister had

45

stumbled on it by accident. Or by the hazard of her wandering life had met them—one of them—all of them —before? So that she had to be removed before the ship reached Bermuda, and was removed, in much the way he had suggested to Sally—a limp body, drugged or slugged—propped up for passers-by, then tipped quickly over the rail.

Tim finished his drink without haste, exchanging a few words with others who came up to the bar while he sat there. Then he left his stool and went out towards the head of the stairs down to B deck. As he moved towards it he saw a light shining through the open door of the writing room. So he changed his mind and went past it, glancing in. Sir John and Lady Meadows were playing bridge with the Bernsteins. The couples were divided. It was impossible to tell how this suited them, whether they liked it, played better or worse, made money or lost it. To stop and watch would be too obviously ill-mannered. So Tim went on, made his way out on deck, leaned on the rail to watch the night, cursed his general lack of success in familiar terms and turning away, swayed on towards his descent to C deck and his own small cabin there.

Sir John Meadows, looking up from his cards, had seen the thin face turned towards him as the journalist passed the open door.

"Newspaper fellow," he said, leaning back as the game, set and rubber came to an end. "Be a good chap, Bernstein, and tot it up. No head for figures."

"Lady Meadows said, "Why did you say 'newspaper fellow', John?"

"Saw him pass the door just now. Which reminds me . . ."

He paused to collect the attention of the others. Max Bernstein looked up from his sums. His wife Lottie suddenly put out her hand to cover his free one.

"Well?" Lady Meadows said. "Go on, John. Reminds you of what?"

"It reminds me of the night before we reached Bermuda. Quite late. I'd left my library book in here and I wanted it. I switched the light on and went in. I heard a noise behind me and turned. Fennister was there with his wife. I think they'd just come up the stairs. They were quite close, outside the door. I don't think they saw me. I was stooping behind one of the writing tables. The stacks of paper would hide me. But I heard him say to her, 'The other side would be best, wouldn't it?' or words to that effect. He had a marked Italian accent, hadn't he?"

There was a pause.

"Was that *all*?" Lady Meadows said, disappointed.

"Yes. They'd gone when I looked up after finding my book. I only heard him say that. I didn't see which way they really went."

Mrs Bernstein lifted her hand from her husband's and said in a strained voice, "Now it is you must say, Max. As I have told you from that morning, it did have an importance. I was quite sure it had an importance."

He lifted the hand she had released.

"What was the time when you saw these people, Sir John?"

"Quite late. Or early, if you like. About two-thirty in the morning. I couldn't sleep. I wanted to read. I remembered I'd left my book—"

"I too," said Max Bernstein, "was restless. I have dreams sometimes. I still have dreams—"

"We do understand," Lady Meadows said in her vague gentle voice, less in sympathy than a fear of being told some horror tale from the war.

"So I went out on deck and stood near the door from the lounge. It was a very dark night. Wild, too. The sea was making a noisy splashing and the movement was strong but it was right for my—my state of mind. Then I saw I was not alone. Further along, in a position to see the whole length of the side of the ship, was a woman. At least I assumed a woman."

"This side or that?" asked Sir John. "I mean port or starboard?"

"That other—port, isn't it?"

"Who was she?" Lady Meadows was tense, very anxious to hear the end of the story.

"I am not even now quite sure," Mr. Bernstein said apologetically. "I did not want to have to speak to her, so I moved on this, the starboard side, to find a door to go in by. As I went forward and then round to my cabin I saw two figures, a woman in a stewardess's uniform I now recognised as that Spanish—"

"Conchita," said Mrs Bernstein, interrupting her husband for the first time. "South American, they tell me."

"And the man?" asked Lady Meadows.

"I cannot be sure," Mr Bernstein told her, frowning. "That is why I have said nothing until now. But it must have been Mr Fennister, I think, since you say he was up at about that time. I was a little later than you. After three."

"But you did not see his wife with him then?"

"No. Only the stewardess."

"And not distressed? Not—agitated?"

"Not at all. But only for a moment. You think we must now report what we saw, Sir John?"

"I wonder if we need."

"Really, John!"

"You may be right, my dear. We might sleep on it, don't you think? What's the damage, Bernstein?"

"*Damage?*" Mr Bernstein winced visibly.

"Bridge. What do we owe you?"

The sum was finished, the amount settled. They said goodnight and parted.

Mrs Fairbrother, finishing her letter to her sister at the furthest table in the room, peeped round the corner of it at the four retreating backs. So the Fennisters had both been on deck in the middle of that strange and tragic night. He had *not* slept right through it and waked to find her gone from her bunk. He had met Conchita too,

48

alone. Or had that been some other man? Mr Bernstein had been uncertain. At any rate no alarm had been given in the night. Nothing until the morning. Very queer. Queerer and queerer, Mrs Fairbrother thought.

She slipped her letter into an envelope, fastened it and put it in her bag. Then she went out of the writing room, leaving the lights as she had found them. In the morning, she decided, she would warn Sally Combes about Conchita.

CHAPTER V

On the lowest deck aft a vigorous tournament of deck tennis singles occupied most of the younger group of passengers. When Sally joined them at mid-morning the early heats had been run off and the second of the men's semi-finals was in progress. She was welcomed with loud, persuading cries.

"Why didn't you come before? We need you!"

"She can stand in for Helen!"

"You've got to make up Helen's pair!"

Sally looked round the circle of faces. Helen, whose surname she had never heard, was the wife of one of the doctors.

"I don't see Helen," she said.

Loud laughter greeted this simple remark.

"That's exactly it! She and Ian won their heat and their semi-final comes up after these two are through. One set, best of five games, we're playing."

The semi-finalists finished their match with one of them flat on his face on the deck, the other doubled up in laughter. Loud applause greeted this tableau and again everyone-yelled at once. Sally waited.

At the end of another hour she found herself something of a heroine. Her partner Ian, whose destination was surgical registrar at a hospital in Jamaica, apologised for dragging her into the game in place of his wife, who had gone away to their cabin with an attack of migraine. He then proceeded to take on the opposing pair with only token assistance from herself. Sometimes, in fact, in spite of her opposition, when he poached too blatantly on her side of the chalk-marked pitch, Sally found it quite easy to understand his wife's migraine, a disease of mixed guilt and self-protection a psychiatrist had once told her, but she had not then believed him. Now she wondered if he might in some instances be right.

"Through to the the finals, thanks to you," Ian said, patting her shoulder kindly as they made way for the men's singles final.

The medical circle made a place for her in their midst. Ian went off to see how his wife was feeling, promising to be back in good time for the doubles final. Sally felt she had already done her duty to the community and could not care less if she never saw him again.

"You mustn't mind Ian," the woman anaesthetist said. "He always gets into a tizz when Helen has one of her migraines. Besides it's the second in the last week. She had one the night before we got to Bermuda."

She caught her breath, remembering for the first time what had happened that night.

"So they were up, but perhaps not about, too," said Sally quietly.

The group was listening now, faces turned to her again as they had been when she came among them.

"As well as poor Mrs Fennister," said Dora Cummins, one of the pair of school teachers who were on their way to Tobago.

"I suppose so," said Sally warily.

"Did you actually come on board with Mr Rogers?" asked another woman. "I mean, are you a journalist as well?"

"How did you find out he was a journalist?" Sally asked. "He seemed to want to keep that a secret. At least he asked me not to spread it."

"Rather typical," answered the woman, whom Sally now identified as the Miss O'Shea at the Captain's table on the first night out from Bermuda. Remembering the rest of that night she could not help wincing. Miss O'Shea misunderstood the sudden spasm of disgust that passed over Sally's face.

51

"They can't help it, you know," she said, kindly. "They wouldn't take up the work if they weren't born hyper-critical and curious."

Sally was bewildered.

"I'm afraid I don't quite—" she began, but another question was flung at her from further off.

"I'm not all that interested in Tim Rogers," the voice said harshly. "What I want to know is why nobody slips a hint to Mrs Longford to lay off the Captain. I know a cruise is supposed to be an opportunity for man hunters, but why must she chase the one individual we depend on for taking us safely across the ocean."

Sally stared. The voice came from beyond the medical circle, from the throat of a stout female sunbathing in far too scanty a bathing dress in the front row of the spectators. Should she explain Mrs Longford's position? Arouse pity for her in her sudden and unexpected family tragedy? It would be a natural thing to do. But she was held back by her memory of Mrs Longford the night before dancing happily and discreetly with Captain Crowthorne. Yes, discreetly enough. And why shouldn't she? Dick had said they were old friends. For a moment she felt inclined to break the interesting news Dick had given her; that Mrs Longford was the drowned woman's sister, who had been travelling with her to South America to help with the Mario Fenestri tour. But she was re-pelled both by the censorious note in the woman's voice and the avid lust for vicarious excitement behind it.

So she turned her head away without speaking and found Ian beside her and the organiser of the tourna-ment waving to them to come forward to play their final.

They won again, this time with a small prize attached and an extra bonus for Ian, who had backed himself to win.

Immediately an outcry arose. At the start of the tourna-ment he had backed himself and Helen, not himself and Sally. So how could he collect with a different partner in two of the matches? Quite simple, Ian explained. He had altered his bet when Helen retired.

As Sally turned away to go up to B deck she met Tim coming down.

"I know that expression," he said, stopping to take her arm and climb the stairs again. "Come across."

She told him about the gossip-mongers and about Ian's rather squalid gambling.

"Far too sensitive," he said smiling. "Come and get your ice—just going round—I was looking for you. Mrs Fairbrother wants us. She's having a whale of a time this morning, being mysterious and cagey and simply longing to give us two the very latest she's picked up."

"I don't know if I really want to hear it," Sally said. "The more we find out the more it looks like suicide. Why can't we leave the poor woman in peace? They can't even begin to look for her body. They aren't looking for it, are they?"

"Don't be morbid," he said firmly.

Mrs Fairbrother was in her usual place. The deck steward was waiting with his tray of ices and his board with the list of entries for the day's run.

"I never win these things," Sally said, writing in her name and her guess and handing over her shilling.

When the man had gone and the two young people were settled beside her Mrs Fairbrother reported what she had heard in the library the night before.

Tim said thoughtfully, "So Mario lied when he said he had slept all night and had not heard his wife leave the cabin."

"Why did he, if he had been on deck with her at two in the morning?" Sally asked.

"Why indeed, unless he meant to put her overboard?" asked Mrs Fairbrother.

"She *could* have gone back later to throw herself over," Tim said frowning. "But it's very unlikely. And then Conchita . . ."

He broke off. Mrs Fairbrother looked significantly at Sally. The girl knew she was waiting for her to tell Tim about the note in Felicity's handwriting. A suicide note if the woman had really written it, a clever forgery if it had been faked to cover a murder.

Disregarding Mrs Fairbrother's unspoken prompting Sally turned to Tim.

"Yes, Conchita," she said. "Haven't you got anything out of her yet? Did she really follow Mr Fennister to Europe? Did she know he and his wife were going to be on board *Selena* for this trip? What's their connection?"

"I have seen her," Tim answered. "Yesterday and this morning. She didn't tell me she saw the Fennisters during the night Felicity disappeared. But she did say something very strange."

"What was that?"

"She asked me—I had accused her of being jealous of the girl—she asked me if I suspected her of murder. I said why should I. She said quite so. She had no motive. Felicity was part of Mario's act. That was the only legal thing in their relationship."

"Indeed," said Mrs Fairbrother. "What about their marriage?"

"That was it," Tim answered. "She implied it was not legal. Because Mario had married her in Brazil twelve years ago."

Married!" both women exclaimed.

"Yes. You may as well know now as later. That was what I found out when I met Conchita by chance in Rio. She had been drinking. It all came oozing out between tears and fresh drinks. Her early career as a dancer. Mario in a not very good trapeze act. Their marriage. His wish to try his luck in Europe again. Her refusal to go with him. Their separation for ten years, until he came back, but only to the West Indies in a new high-wire act with a brilliant girl."

"Felicity!"

"Just so. She heard of it, saw photographs, wrote, but got no answer. She followed his tour but never had enough money to reach him before he went back to Europe.

54

Now she was going to follow."

"As a stewardess?"

"Actually I suggested that as a way to follow," Tim said. He did not look disturbed by the apparent consequences of his suggestion. But Sally was horrified.

"So all this may really be *your* responsibility," she gasped.

Even Mrs Fairbrother protested.

"No, no, my dear. Don't exaggerate. Tim was only trying to be helpful. Was, in fact, very helpful. Anyway, we can't discuss consequences with hindsight. It is always a pointless exercise. No. But we can discuss what happened in the light of Tim's facts."

"You mean knowing Felicity wasn't really Mario's wife and Conchita was?" Sally tried to review the position calmly. "So what? She had only to claim him and prove it."

"It was registered in Rio. I took care to verify it before I flew to Bermuda to come on board *Selena*," Tim said soberly.

"Right," Sally went on. "They met and recognised each other, I presume?"

"Conchita says so."

"She was going to confront them together? Or what was she going to do?"

"She was going to get Mario back but she did not want to break up the act. It was too valuable."

"Good God!" said Mrs Fairbrother. For the first time she looked really shocked.

"It's understandable," said Tim. "He's doing very nicely. Lining up with Felicity was a godsend for him."

"But then—then—neither Mario nor Conchita would really want to kill Felicity," Sally said, breathlessly. "But Felicity must have been appalled when she knew. Mustn't she?"

Neither Tim nor Mrs Fairbrother agreed at once.

"If she was in love with her husband," Mrs Fairbrother then said slowly, "she would want to get rid of Conchita, not the other way round. The—the stewardess—was in the strong position, wasn't she? But she could still be very jealous—even murderously jealous. Not capable of reasoning. She is South American, isn't she? Peon?"

"Probably," Tim answered. "A Latin-Indian temper. I've seen it. But perhaps Latin avarice as well. Mario has money now. If the act was broken he would be back where he started."

"The act *is* broken," Sally said.

That grim fact could not be denied. Whatever the actual motives, the actual facts, that at least was certain.

Mrs Fairbrother waved a hand impatiently.

"The future does not concern us," she said. "Oh, I'm sorry for Mr Fennister, provided of course he did not kill his wife. But it would seem he is not suspected. The Bermudan police came aboard, you know. I saw two of them, both uniformed. They were with Captain Crowthorne for quite a time, I believe. I expect they saw Mrs Longford as well."

"The Bermudan police had nothing whatever to say to me," Tim added. "Nor had they to the paper I'm doing this job for."

Sally was tired of the problem. Quite suddenly she felt she could not bear to hear the name of Mario Fenestri one single time more. She got up briskly.

"I'm for a swim," she said. "Coming in, Tim?"

"Maybe," he answered. "I'm behind with my notes. Don't wait for me."

As if I would, Sally thought, as she went along to her cabin.

In the late afternoon of that day there was a cricket match between passengers and crew, held on that part of the deck where the tennis tournament had been played in the morning.

Sally watched from above, with much the same group of younger women who had been playing or watching the tennis. Their men were below, taking part in the cricket match.

"Passengers always lose," her next-door neighbour said. "I believe the captains of cruise ships coach their teams in secret."

"I can't think where," Sally answered, laughing.

She saw she was speaking to Helen, Ian's wife.

"The migraine has gone, I hope," she said.

Helen frowned.

"It was really bad. I wanted to stay for our semi-finals, but Ian wouldn't let me."

"I expect he thought you weren't up to it," Sally said unthinkingly.

"Because he'd backed us to win, you mean?" Helen said stiffly.

It was exactly what she had meant, but she had not intended Helen to understand this. Rather red in the face she struggled to find some convincing words of denial, but was saved by the progress of the game. Reg, the missionary, by far the strongest bat so far produced by the passengers, had not only beaten the ball over the netting into the sea, but had lost his grip of the bat in doing so. It sailed after the ball into the waves. There was loud applause, the Captain's team of stalwart fielders clapping wildly and turning to look up at the mostly female audience on the deck above.

Sally found herself directly above Dick Groves who was bowling and had turned to pick up a new ball.

"Well bowled!" she called down, for the missionary's effort rated a double penalty and ended his innings.

Dick smiled back and was so much encouraged by her praise that he took the next passenger's wicket with a hard straight ball and the following one from a catch neatly held by Captain Crowthorne.

"Passengers always lose," Tim said at Sally's elbow.

She looked at him with indulgent scorn.

"Don't you play *any* games?" she asked. "You missed out on the tennis this morning and now this."

"Ageing frame out of practice," Tim said grinning, but there was little mirth in his smile.

57

"Rot," said Sally briskly. "Look at the old boy who's in now. Oh, well played!"

A round of applause greeted a hit worth two runs. The middle-aged Yorkshireman, who had been tried once in his youth for the county team, wiped his face with a large handkerchief and addressed himself to the game again.

But the crew did, of course, win and Sally moved away from the group of spectators with Tim still at her side.

"Come and have a drink," he said. "I forgive you for your harsh words."

"Too kind," she answered. "I ought to give you a drink to make amends. I must just get a cardigan. It cools too fast after the sun goes down."

He followed her to the door of her cabin. She unlocked it and went in and immediately stepped back with a cry of mixed anger and fright.

Tim looked quickly up and down the corridor then pushed Sally into the cabin, stepped in after her and shut the door.

"I see," he said, unnecessarily.

The cause of the girl's upset was very plain. The drawers of the dressing table had been emptied on to the floor. The bedding had been thrown back from the bed, from both beds. Even the little cupboard below the mirror in the bathroom had been pulled open and its contents lay scattered in the washbasin.

"Looking for—what?" asked Tim, slowly.

Sally moved to the wall and pressed the bell marked 'Stewardess'.

"I know what she wanted," she said. "What I don't understand and don't much like is why advertise the search?"

Tim stared.

"You may be right at that. I'll be in the bar," he said and was gone.

Sally sat down on the side of her bunk. No one came.

She rang again. The same young man who had attended her on her first night aboard came at last, gasping audibly as he saw the havoc, with Sally sitting tense and white-faced in the middle of it.

"Someone has gone mad in my cabin," she said. "Where is Conchita?"

"Off duty," he stammered.

"Go and tell her what you have seen. In five minutes I shall report this to the Chief Steward."

"He is off duty," the man said sullenly.

"I shall report it," she repeated.

He went away. As she expected, in less than five minutes Conchita arrived, outraged, mystified, full of indignation and theories. The main theory, to which she recurred several times was that the journalist, meaning Tim, had done it.

"He came to snoop after Senora Fenestri she disappear, she drown."

"I think that is most unlikely. He was with me when I found my cabin in this state. He was just as surprised and shocked as I am."

For a moment she hesitated. Had Tim really been surprised? Really shocked? His behaviour and speech had been laconic. But then they usually were. A disillusioned character. Disappointed too. Cynical.

She found Conchita staring at her, still defiant, still ready to find explanations. The whole thing was ridiculous.

"You may help me to tidy up," she said. "I will check and you can put away. If anything has been taken I will make a note of it. But I think nothing has been taken. I think the madman or madwoman who did this . . ."

Conchita, on her knees by the dressing table, folding and stowing away the scattered clothes, stopped to cross herself, looking up sideways at Sally.

"It could be—it is possible—a spirit did this. An unhappy spirit. In mortal sin— This suicide—"

59

"Nonsense!" said Sally briskly. "Superstitious nonsense."

Her patience had suddenly snapped. Knowing what she did and believing what Tim had told her, this pantomime was absurd.

Conchita gave her a savage glance but made no answer. In silence they restored the cabin to its former tidy condition.

"I go now," Conchita said at the end. She seemed subdued, tired, in some way shaken by the failure of her suggestions and hints, which she must have realised had made no impression whatever on the cold self-contained English girl.

"Yes, go now," Sally said. "I will not complain this time, but if anything of the sort happens again I shall go straight to the Captain."

This roused the stewardess a little.

"You go if you like," she said with a little of her former fire. "As if I care! I leave at Barbados. Tomorrow, I leave."

Sally joined Tim in the bar. He had a chair ready for her beside a small corner table.

"I thought you were never coming," he said. "I was wondering if she'd cut your throat."

"She'd have liked to," Sally answered. "Old-fashioned martini, please. How did you know I'd sent for her?"

"Obvious, wasn't it? A kind of warning off, I suppose."

"In a way. But I'd like you to read this."

She took Felicity's note from her bag. It had been undisturbed in its place in her locked suitcase under the spare bunk.

Tim read it and handed it back.

"Genuine suicide note or rather crude fake?" he asked.

"I don't know. The writing, according to Captain Crowthorne, is genuine."

"I see."

"I don't. I don't see anything in this business that

isn't puzzling, sinister and thoroughly foul."

"Perhaps. Or just a simple tale of jealousy and greed."

"That's what I meant by foul."

The conversation languished. Other passengers stopped to talk to them. A game of bingo after dinner was proposed by the medical group. Sally agreed to join, Tim opted out.

The bingo went on longer than Sally expected but she got away as soon as it was over, had a shower and got into bed, where she lay looking up at the ceiling and thinking over the strange wrecking of her cabin.

It was then that she noticed the scratches in the paint, not only on the ceiling but on the walls as well. Roused by these strange signs of damage she got up again to inspect them more closely. It was a long time, even after she later turned out her light, before she managed to sleep. She took Tim to her cabin directly after breakfast the next morning to show him her new finds.

"A struggle?" she suggested. "A fight? You said she must have been dead or unconscious if she was actually put overboard to drown."

"Did I?" Tim seemed even more laconic than usual this morning. "Yes, I must have."

"Well, what d'you think?"

"I think," he said, smiling gently, "that they must have been practising their act, or parts of it, in here and chipped the paint doing it."

"Their act!" Sally was indignant and at the same time felt she might have let her imagination go too far.

"They had to keep in practice, hadn't they? It would have been difficult to do it publicly. But a few hand-springs— They could rig a practice wire, I suppose. It doesn't have to be much above the ground. The balancing is the same wherever you do it—"

"Then you don't think—"

He moved away to the door.

"I think you'd better give up making theories, Sally," he said. "About the Fennisters, anyway. Probably about

61

Conchita, too."

"Oh, Conchita," Sally said carelessly. "I've written her off. She's leaving us at Barbados. She told me so."

"Is she indeed?" Tim said, pausing as he left the cabin. "Now that really *is* something."

CHAPTER VI

Selena berthed in Bridgetown, Barbados, at dawn on the following morning. Many of the passengers watched the approach from an early hour, but Sally, tired after two late and disturbed nights and much puzzling over the Fennister mystery, overslept and did not go down to breakfast until that meal, also laid early, was nearly over.

She reached her place to find Tim Rogers just getting up to leave.

"What's the hurry?" she asked, still feeling bemused, for she had woken to find the ship at rest and a variety of shore noises assailing her, noises that had grown unfamiliar in a week at sea.

"We sail again this evening. I'm off ashore. Be seeing you."

He was gone, the dining saloon was emptying fast, but the table steward was at her elbow, so Sally pulled herself together and ordered her usual breakfast which she ate without much enthusiasm.

At the Purser's desk a small queue had lined up to get local currency for shopping on shore. Most of those who had decided to see something of Bridgetown had provided themselves in this way the day before and were already assembling on the deck.

Selena was alongside the quay, her gangway lowered and fixed. The passengers gathered themselves into parties and trooped down to a swarm of waiting taxis.

Mrs Fairbrother stood near the rail watching them go. She had planned a little excursion for Trinidad on the following day but was staying on board that morning. So she leaned on the rail and watched with an amused smile on her lips and an occasional word for those passengers who usually kept her company on deck.

The noisy Yorkshire party left very early. They were already off the ship by the time Mrs Fairbrother took up her position. Also very early to leave, but plainly recognisable, was the dark stewardess from B deck whose name, Sally Combes had told her, was Conchita. She was wearing a very smart, very tight-fitting, very short-skirted dress in a red, orange and green floral pattern and she carried a large suitcase. Mrs Fairbrother noticed that the Chief Steward had appeared at the head of the gangway a few minutes before Conchita arrived. The stewardess saw him but moved forward, keeping her eyes fixed on the shore. He stepped in front of her.

"You have all your belongings in the bag, Conchita?" he asked calmly.

"Of course."

Her voice and look were insolent. She could not have made her freedom, her independence, more positive.

"Then I will say goodbye on behalf of Captain Crowthorne and the rest of the ship's company. I hope you will find your husband as you expect."

She gave him a quick glance.

"What does that mean? You have news by radio? You have not told me?"

He shrugged very slightly.

"I mean I don't see him waiting down there. But perhaps you don't expect him to meet you on the wharf."

That she had expected this was clear from the sudden anxiety in her eyes, her quick frown. But she did not go to the rail to look. She only held out her hand to shake his politely, say goodbye formally and picking up her suitcase go gingerly down the gangway, swaying a little on her high-heeled black sandals.

Mrs Fairbrother had not heard this conversation but she guessed its content, for she had herself watched the crowd below very closely and had found no one remotely like Mario or his manservant who was his dresser, or the impresario who had received the acrobat at Bermuda with cries and despair and sympathy and anger and again despair.

Sir John Meadows lowered his head to emerge from the door near the gangway. He was followed by Lady Meadows, who walked over to Mrs Fairbrother.

"John insists upon exploring," she said. "I'm not going and I don't believe you are either."

"No. No, I'm not," Mrs Fairbrother agreed. She spoke vaguely and had not looked at Lady Meadows because her eyes were fastened on the former stewardess who had hesitated, brushing off the appeals of the taxi drivers and looking about her in a distracted fashion. What chiefly intrigued Mrs Fairbrother was her bird's-eye view of the scene, which showed her Tim, the journalist, half hidden to her, wholly hidden from Conchita, but who now moved to watch her. When Conchita began to walk on, going slowly away still carrying her suitcase, Tim moved out to follow her and the pair soon disappeared from view round the corner of the big customs shed.

It was at this point that Mrs Fairbrother noticed the bridge players. They were standing beside a large Cadillac, talking earnestly to a couple of prosperous looking Barbadians in white suits, flowered shirts open at the neck and white and brown shoes. The argument was short, ending abruptly. All the men piled into the car, one of the local couple took the driver's seat, the other waved them away. After which he walked down to the quayside to spit thoughtfully into the water before climbing into a small red three-wheeler parked among some motor scooters. In a moment he too was gone.

Sally, quite alone in the dining saloon at the end of her breakfast, except for the stewards who were setting the other tables for the next meal, decided that it was too late to go ashore. She went up to the Purser's desk to find the news sheet and sat reading it listlessly for nearly twenty minutes, although she had absorbed the headlines in five. After that she went to her cabin to write letters, but found it occupied by the cabin steward, working fast for he had been given shore leave and Sally's late rising had held him up.

She apologised when she understood the situation, which he made very clear in terms bordering upon insolence. But her spirits were too low for her to resent his behaviour. In fact she was not really aware of it and went away to write her letters in the library, leaving him startled and a little apprehensive at her calm indifference.

Letter writing offered some relief to her feelings but left Sally wondering why she had minded so much being left behind on board when nearly all the passengers had gone ashore. Examining her state more closely she was honest enough to realise that it was Tim's behaviour that had hurt. If his plan for the day was purely professional why not warn her the night before? If not, was it so urgent, so necessary to go early? Or had he made an arrangement with some other girl? He had seemed to single herself out for his attentions, but had she really taken the trouble to do more than accept them, enjoy them and expect—what?

They were not children, she told herself solemnly. Certainly Tim was no child. He was a somewhat disappointed young man who had tried a variety of jobs and found little satisfaction so far in any of them. Freelance journalism was a precarious position to reach at thirty or thereabouts. Perhaps his ambition was greater than his ability, she told herself sagely. It comforted her bruised ego to run him down to herself. At twenty-two she considered her judgements mature.

She began to run over her several violent friendships with men. With boys, rather, she corrected herself honestly. These affairs had flowered and fallen very rapidly. They had been experimental but not alarmingly so. As fellow students at the university both sides had wished to appear modern but not aggressively avant-garde. Secretly both she and the boy-friends, as in each case she ultimately discovered, were sufficiently intel-

66

gent and interested in their work to shy away from
isks that might prevent them getting their degrees. Tim
Rogers had no degree, or she had heard of none.

"Really you know very little about Tim Rogers, my
ear," Mrs Fairbrother said, when later that morning
ally sat beside her in the shade, fanning herself with
er writing block and licking her ice-cream slowly.

"I know," she answered. She would have liked to add
'and care less" but it would be too obviously untrue.

Mrs Fairbrother had been telling the girl about her
musing time watching people go ashore from the
ecently berthed ship. She spoke of Sir John and the
Yorkshire contingent and of the card players whose names
10 one seemed to know but whom most people now
avoided.

"Nothing really bad, I believe," she said. "But one or
wo have asked me if they ought to complain to the
Captain after they'd lost a good deal of money to them.
But I told them it was none of the poor Captain's fault,
1or could he do anything about it. It was their own
ault for playing for high stakes."

"Did you actually tell them that?"

"Well—no," Mrs Fairbrother answered laughing. "I
nade it quite clear what I thought, though."

Sally frowned.

"I've been watching them lately, too," she said. "I
hink the way they always get together near the bar
s rather sinister. They just arrive, order drinks, settle
lown and may not say a word for ages. They never call
each other anything."

"Do you mean they never speak any names when they
are talking?"

"Yes. I mean no. Never. That's why nobody knows
who they are."

"Oh, but we can find out," Mrs Fairbrother said,
ishing in the large cream-coloured leather handbag she
took about with her. She brought up the printed passenger list, opened it and drew a finger down the names.

"You must have one too," she told Sally.

The girl remembered it. She had found it on her dressing table the day they had sailed. She had left it there. now she leaned over to read the list Mrs Fairbrother hel

"The school teachers and the missionaries leave at Trinidad," she said.

"But that's tomorrow," Sally exclaimed.

"Well, yes. Why so surprised?"

"I've only just got to know them."

Mrs Fairbrother smiled. For all her air of sophistic tion and quiet competence the girl was very youn quite a child in some ways.

"Then the Bahamas. Yes, the doctors leave there. A look, these three. No, four. All men."

"I thought the doctors were going to Jamaica."

"So they are. But *Selena* doesn't call there. They fly from Nassau, I expect."

"So those are the four—"

"We haven't finished yet. Bermuda. Your T Rogers—"

"He isn't my Tim Rogers," Sally said, laughing last. "I see he leaves at Bermuda. And I do, too. I' supposed to be flying home from there. The Bernstei are getting off at Bermuda, aren't they?"

"So they told me," Mrs Fairbrother said. "She nev likes to be away from England for long, he said. Ve restless. Her war experiences, perhaps. Or before tha They got out to the Channel Islands, you know, in 19; and then had to run again, poor things. Almost pennile by that time."

"They aren't penniless now," Sally could not hel saying.

"No, bless them," said Mrs Fairbrother, comfortab relieved of the necessity for pity. "They keep the knac don't they? Of hard work and money wisdom and that

"So no one has actually left the ship here," Sally sai leaning back in her chair again.

"None of the passengers, according to our list," M

Fairbrother corrected her. "But your stewardess has gone. We shan't see *her* again."

She described Conchita's appearance and behaviour. Sally was not surprised and said so. Mrs Fairbrother nodded wisely. It bore out all the gossip had told them hitherto.

"But you say no one was on shore to meet her?" Sally asked after a pause for thought.

"No. She waited for a bit and then walked slowly away round the corner of one of the big sheds."

"The last of Conchita," said Sally.

But she was wrong.

Selena was due to sail at half past four that afternoon. An hour before this the sight-seeing crowd of passengers trooped on board, greeted at the head of the gangway by those friends who had not ventured ashore for such a short excursion. They came walking slowly, laden with parcels, hot and dishevelled, or driving in taxis, cool, unhurried, their parcels borne up the gangway by drivers who had earned already double fares and generous tips.

The bridge players arrived together, poker-faced as usual, but alone in an ordinary taxi. Sally identified them easily, but had forgotten their names. In any case she would not have known which was which. She wondered why they had lost the escorts Mrs. Fairbrother had described, the Cadillac that had taken them from the wharf and the little red three-wheeler that had taken away the last to leave.

Sally was standing at the rail watching all this when she heard her name called. She turned to find Dick Groves just behind her.

"Been ashore?" he asked cheerfully. He moved to the rail and looked over, searching the crowd below.

"No," she answered. It sounded ungracious and a bit resentful, she thought, so she added, "I'm going to have a proper trip tomorrow in Trinidad. We shan't have to be back so perishingly early, shall we?"

He laughed at her vehemence.

"No."

She waited for an explanation, but none was forthcoming. Dick moved back a little.

"I'm supposed to be counting them in," he said, smiling. "I'll have to check. Don't go away."

She stayed where she was, watching Dick, no longer interested in the thinning procession moving on board. He was talking to the Chief Steward and the Second Officer both of whom were at the door that led in from the deck, while a couple of seamen, dressed for the occasion in white smocks and trousers, stood ready to dismantle the gangway.

So the girl did not see Conchita's arrival at the ship, running, panting, her hair flying, her dress stained with sweat, her high-heeled shoes in one hand with her handbag in the other, her suitcase bumping against her as she ran.

But Sally saw her as she reached the deck and leaned, breathless, against the rail, quite close to where she stood.

"Conchita!" she cried loudly. "We thought—"

But Dick arrived in a swift bound from where he had been standing. He cut off Sally's view, her intended offer of help, the dark woman's answer if she made one. Then the other two officers closed in and before any of the last of the passengers could turn round, the commotion was over. Conchita with the Chief Steward and the Second Officer were walking briskly forward. Dick, left behind, turned to Sally.

"She has come back," he said. "She did not find her husband. He was not here."

"Did you know that?"

"Not until after she'd gone ashore. At least, I don't think so."

Sally remembered the cold faces of the bridge players and shivered. Then she said, "Everyone else has come back, then?"

"Not quite."

70

He was looking at her with open curiosity. Sally resented it. She had not seen Tim. So Tim had not come back.

"Who's missing then?" she asked casually.

"The journalist," he said, still watching her. "We've given him an extra ten minutes and he's not back, so I'm afraid he's boobed."

Bells rang. Orders were given. The engines woke from their dozing murmurs, the ship began to tremble, the seamen raised the gangway. Sally shrugged, writing off Tim Rogers without any remaining pang. There was always Dick Groves, more her age and really very attractive.

At dinner that night Tim's place was empty. There had been no new passengers boarding at Barbados, the Chief Officer told them. He had not heard that the journalist was leaving. Perhaps he had been left behind by his own fault. The Chief Officer did not specify what might have kept him.

Nora Ford suggested drink. The rest of the table, who had other ideas, made no suggestions.

It was a dull meal. Sally, in spite of her revised attitude towards Tim, missed his cheerful conversation and preposterous anecdotes. The Chief Officer suggested that he might join them again at Trinidad. There were frequent flights between the islands.

"You mean if he just missed the boat?" one of the others asked.

"Yes."

As no one was sufficiently interested to enlarge on this theory the subject was dropped finally and the rest of the meal passed in what for Sally was a dreary catalogue of the merits and demerits of Bridgetown as a holiday shopping centre.

She spent the next part of the evening with the Fords, the Cumminses and Phyllis O'Shea, who joined her colleagues in the lounge. All of them were leaving the ship at Port of Spain, the teachers to go on to Tobago and the missionary pair to Haiti. They all seemed a little over-excited, Sally thought. The high purposes with which they had set out still upheld them, but reality was creeping up fast. Though they had not gone ashore at Bridgetown, their table discussion being at second hand, all of them had spent most of the day watching the busy unfamiliar activities on the wharfside. Much of the behaviour there had been startlingly alien, the English patois unintelligible. They realised at last that far from handing out knowledge of learning and of God they were about to undergo the most challenging course of instruction they had met so far in their young, or in the case of Miss O'Shea, not so young, lives.

Feeling tired after her totally idle day Sally did not stay in this company for long. She had taken a new book from the library that morning. She decided to go to bed and read. But as she walked across the lounge she saw Mrs Fairbrother beckoning to her. The old lady was sitting with the Newbuckles.

"We wanted to ask you if you had fixed up with a party to see something of Trinidad," Mrs Fairbrother said.

Sally explained quite truthfully that she had not given it a thought.

"We wondered if you'd give us the pleasure of joining us," Fred Newbuckle said formally in his deep voice. "Mabel thought as so many of the young people are leaving . . ."

"Fred and I want to go across to Maracas beach," Mrs Newbuckle said. "So if you are free . . ."

"I have friends in Port of Spain," Mrs Fairbrother said, unexpectedly. "Otherwise . . ."

Sally looked at the kind, complacent faces and hated them all. She registered another mark against Tim Rogers. But the sudden realisation that to refuse this offer would probably mean another unsupportable blistering day on board in harbour made up her mind for her at once.

"Thank you," she said, forcing a smile. "Thank you very much. I'd love to come."

Mabel Newbuckle sighed her relief.

"We ought to start early," she said.

Mrs Fairbrother laughed.

"I told Mabel you got up very late today," she said. "But I expect you'll be early tomorrow. We'll be going in through the Dragon's Teeth or the Serpent's Mouth if the weather's right, Captain Crowthorne says. Very spectacular."

"What time?" Fred Newbuckle asked.

"Just before dawn. Between five and six."

"Too early for me," he shuddered.

Sally felt challenged.

"I might if I wake up," she said carelessly. "But I won't be late for going ashore," she added and said good-night and walked away.

What an old know-all Mrs Fairbrother is, she thought. Never at a loss. Friends in Port of Spain. Confidences from the Captain. Or perhaps just something he said at dinner. In which case the Newbuckles knew it too, though Fred didn't seem to. What did it matter? What did anything matter on this boring cruise with all these boring people. It was most unlikely she would wake up before dawn.

CHAPTER VII

But she did. She slept fitfully all night, looking at her watch on each awakening, turning off her light each time, determined not to rouse herself again and each time turning on the light once more to discover how long she had slept since the last time.

She got up at half past five, dressed quickly and went out into the silent corridor. The Purser's desk was shuttered, the space before it empty. But as she turned from it, half decided to go back to bed, the door leading to the deck was pushed open and Nora Ford came in, white-faced and breathless.

"Hullo," Sally said, relieved to find someone else up as foolish as herself. "You've beaten me to it. Is it worth going out to see?"

"Horrible!" Nora gasped. "It—it's horrible!"

"What is?"

Sally, though startled, was sceptical. Nora, she had found, was inclined to dislike anything unfamiliar and to describe it in exaggerated terms. Flying fish for breakfast she had considered horrible. So now Sally quickly suppressed a vision of drowned corpses or similar disasters and said, "You're scared, Nora! What is it?"

"Out *there!*" the girl said, pointing to the door. "So close! Enormous! I . . ."

"Show me," Sally said, putting an arm round Nora and drawing her back on to the deck.

The darkness outside was of two kinds and Sally at once understood her companion's fear. The sky above was dark but sprinkled with stars; the water beneath the ship was dark, shot with lines of silver phosphorescence. But directly before her, that is along the length of the ship as she stood with her hands now clutching the rail, was a totally black mass rising to a jagged edge, a mass so near she felt she could reach a hand to touch it as the ship swept by.

"It's only a rock," she said, trying to control her voice. "One of those Dragon's Teeth they were talking about yesterday. Or weren't you there?"

"I thought," Nora said in a very subdued voice, "I thought we were going to run into it. I was going to find Reg."

"And we'd drown together, darling." The missionary's voice came from behind them. He put his arms round his wife who hid her face against his shoulder. "Magnificent, isn't it?" he said to Sally.

"It must be dangerous to go so close," Nora said in a muffled voice.

"I think Captain Crowthorne knows his business," he answered, still holding her close.

The sky was growing lighter all the time, the stars fading. The rock too was further off; they were leaving it behind and a dim outline growing in the distance showed where the shores of Trinidad curved away south.

By this time a few more passengers had appeared, yawning, unimpressed by the semi-darkness, though now a much lighter patch was spreading in the east. The newcomers went forward purposefully; most of them had their cameras and light meters hanging round their necks.

Reg said, "I expect we're allowed up on top as we were passing the Azores."

"On top?" Sally did not understand.

"Come on. We'll show you."

With her husband's presence and the arrival of daylight Nora had recovered. Sally went with them, first to A deck and then, moving beyond the permitted part of the deck, to the staircase behind the bridge that took them to the topmost deck of all. Alone there, her head tied up in a becoming shrimp-coloured scarf was Mrs Longford, levelling her binoculars on the distant shore.

She paid no attention to the small crowd slowly gathering around her. But when Sally left the missionaries to walk across to a point beside her she said "Good-morning. You've made the effort," in a friendly voice.

The remark did not demand an answer but Sally found herself resenting the slightly patronising tone she heard in it.

"I hope it'll be worth it," she said coldly.

"Oh yes, it's sure to be worth it," Mrs Longford told her. Then, offering the glasses she said, "Would you like to look? The sun will make too much glare when it comes up over the mountains. But just now . . ."

Sally took the glasses. She was unfamiliar with such things but her uncle had tried in Bermuda to teach her how to handle them. Without getting a very clear view she fiddled convincingly and then handed them back.

"You've been here before then?" she asked. It was the first time she had spoken to Mrs Longford except as one of a group. She thought the general assumption about her was stupid. If the woman knew Captain Crowthorne why should she not talk to him at other than meal times? Who cared anyway what two middle-aged people did? The old-fashioned, sniggering gossip on this ship was pitiful to say the least.

"Yes," Mrs Longford answered.

Sally wanted to know very much if those other visits had been made with her sister, the lost acrobat. She tried to think of some way to find out but her courage failed. A direct question would only elicit a straight yes or no, as her last question had done. So she stood there dumb, watching the slow approach of Port of Spain, noticing the pause to take up the pilot, the slackened speed as they closed the lines of buoys on either side.

Just before the ship began the manoeuvre of berthing Mrs Longford, who had continued to survey the shore at intervals through her binoculars, took their strap over her head a second time to hand them to Sally.

"You are expecting Tim Rogers to join us again here, I expect," she said. "Well, he has just come down to the wharf. About the middle of that group of immigration and customs officers waiting to come aboard us."

Sally looked, saw nothing but a blur, twiddled the knobs, looked with one eye at the result, saw vague figures and gave it up.

"Yes," she said, confused by her failure and by the news. "I thought he might be here. How did you know?"

Mrs Longford took back the glasses and smiled.

"Breakfast next," she said and turning walked away.

Before going down to the dining saloon however she spoke to Captain Crowthorne, who had come out from the bridge for a minute to say goodbye to the pilot.

"She isn't really expecting him," she said.

"How d'you know?"

It was Sally's question but this time Mrs Longford answered it.

"I told her he was on the quay and handed her the glasses. She pretended she saw him but it was a surprise to her."

"Pretended?"

"Yes. He wasn't there of course. She couldn't have seen him."

"Then why—"

"Because she can't focus binoculars and is too proud to acknowledge it."

"Did you know that before you told her he was there?"

"Naturally. I tried her with them earlier. She handed them back set so impossibly I knew she had been trying to adjust and failed completely."

"You are too clever, Ann," he said coldly and disappeared again on to the bridge.

Sir John and Lady Meadows had not turned out to see the approach to Port of Spain but they were in the dining saloon for breakfast before any of the rest of the Captain's table appeared.

"Will you go ashore here?" she asked him in a low voice.

"I must, since I failed in Bridgetown."

"Won't it be even worse? I mean—"

"You had better come with me. After all, your family connections—"

"I didn't want to impose on them. Not that they need know . . ."

"Exactly." He raised his voice. "Fruit, my dear? Scrambled egg as usual?" The table steward was beside them. Sir John ordered.

The Newbuckles arrived and took their places. Sally, who saw them come in interrupted her own meal to go over to them.

"Down already?" Mr Newbuckle said. "You have the advantage of us."

"I was up before six. The Dragon's Teeth—"

"Serpent's Mouth—"

"Either, isn't it? Anyway, quite exciting."

"You haven't finished yet, have you, Sally?" Mrs Newbuckle asked. "Because I'm not going to let Fred hurry or he'll get indigestion on the drive. His ulcer—"

"You leave my ulcer alone, old lady," her husband ordered.

Sally nodded and went back to her table. She did not mind at all that her expedition would set off later than she expected. It was not going to be much fun spending a whole day with the Newbuckles, kind as they were. It would be interesting to see something of Trinidad; the tropical scene, the poui trees, brilliant yellow on the hillsides, the weaver birds and their long hanging nests, the many-coloured parrots, the craggy northern shore, the pounding surf in Maracas Bay. She had heard so much of these wonders already from passengers who had been here before or were coming back to their homes on the island that she wondered if she would find the magic evaporated when she was actually where she expected it. It would be different if Tim . . . But he had gone away at Bridgetown without a word of his plans, so now, even if he was on the quay, which she had not been able to prove. . . . She poured herself a second cup of coffee, miserably humiliated by her failure with the binoculars, her earlier childish reluctance to get her uncle to show her how to use them properly.

"Still guzzling?" Tim Rogers said, dropping into his former seat beside her. "I'm starving."

The table steward had come rapidly to his side. While Tim ordered a very full breakfast Sally pulled herself together.

"I was up early," she said. "They told me the entrance was pretty spectacular and so it was. Great rocks at arm's length away and pitch black. Super. Fantastic."

"I envy you," Tim said, turning to her as the steward hurried away. "I flew in."

"I suppose so."

"I was held up in Bridgetown. I made the harbour just in time to see *Selena*'s stern leaving the wharf."

"Bad luck."

"Did you think I'd abandoned the job?"

She stared at him, her heart beating uncomfortably fast.

"I didn't really think about you at all," she said untruthfully.

"Liar."

Sally drank the rest of her coffee and got up.

"Don't go," Tim said. "Aren't you surprised at all, not the least bit, to see me back?"

"I knew you were back. I saw you on the quayside."

Tim swallowed his astonishment less successfully than she had hers.

"When did you see me?"

"As we came alongside. I was up on top as you might have known if you'd looked." His expression was so incredulous that she added, "I looked at you through a pair of binoculars."

"Did you indeed? Whose?"

79

"Mrs Longford's. She spotted you first."

Tim's face changed, first to a sudden understanding, and then to puzzlement and finally to a smile of such tender derision that Sally had to turn her head away to hide her quick stab of joy. Again she began to get up and again Tim stopped her, this time with a hand on her arm.

"Have a heart! There are things I must tell you."

She did not sit down again but she did not move away either.

"Well, they can wait. But listen, I've booked a car for us to do a bit of sightseeing." He saw her face change and said, "Don't tell me you're booked already! That old busybody—"

"If you mean Mrs Fairbrother, she's got some sort of assignment with friends who live here. No," She bent over him, speaking almost in a whisper. "It's with the Newbuckles. I can't possibly get out of it."

"Why not?"

She did not bother to answer this. There were several reasons, apart from ordinary consideration for other people's feelings. The most important being a wish to show Tim she was not at his beck and call. She straightened up and this time he did not try to hold her. With a smile to the Newbuckles who, she saw, had reached the toast and marmalade stage of their breakfast she went back to her cabin to get ready for the drive.

When she reached the deck again she found Fred Newbuckle with Tim beside him, waiting at the top of the gangway. As in Barbados passengers were flocking off the ship, while below taxi-drivers shouted their willingness to go anywhere on demand.

"Tim here says he's already fixed up a car," Fred said. "He wants us all to join him, which seems a sensible proposition. If Mabel would show up we could get going."

Mrs Newbuckle's voice assailed them from behind "What are we waiting for?" she cried cheerfully.

"You!" they answered in unison.

"Nonsense," she told them and taking Sally's arm said, "We'll lead the way, dear. Men are such gossips, aren't they?"

The expedition was most successful from a tourist point of view, Sally decided. Wonderful scenery, marvellous rum punches at the County Club, an excellent lunch. Rather to her surprise Tim insisted upon paying his share and hers, in spite of opposition from Mr Newbuckle, who clearly enjoyed playing the host and could obviously well afford it. She made one feeble attempt at independence but Mabel Newbuckle put a stop to it with her usual insensitive common-sense.

"Your young man's working for a paper, isn't he?" she said. "So expenses are expenses. I went through it, though not in newspapers, in the old days myself. As Fred always says, a bit of leniency over expenses goes a long way. You don't get the best out of a chap in your employ if he's miserable through not affording to show off now and then to his girl."

Sally winced but said nothing. To herself she swore she was not Tim's girl and was damned if she ever would be. He had not tried to get away with her from the others for a single minute during the whole day, in spite of one or two careful movements she had made to make it easy for him to do so. He couldn't have anything of much importance to tell her, she decided.

As the four of them parted at the top of the gangway with thanks all round Tim said to Sally, "I'd like to suggest something for tonight, but I've got to hang about. Conchita went ashore again this morning early. I've got to see if she stays ashore this time or if she comes back again. She's supposed to have left now for good. You do understand, don't you, love?"

"To hell with Conchita!" said Sally furiously and marched away. Calling her 'love', copying the Newbuckles' way of addressing each other, was the last straw. She wished she could leave this dreadful ship with its sordid mystery and its scandalmongers and fly back to

81

Bermuda. She remembered with shame and regret tha
she had failed to say goodbye to the teachers and mis
sionaries. All because bloody know-all Tim had come
back. She tried to turn her thoughts to Dick, even to look
forward to seeing him in the lounge that evening. But he
had gone on shore leave early and was on watch now
she learned by some roundabout questions. She was back
with Mrs Fairbrother, who kept her talking and listen
ing until quite late. The bridge players had gone ashore
and not returned, the old lady told her. Several new pas
sengers would join the ship the next day. *Selena* would
remain in port, re-fuelling she understood until just afte
lunch.

"Our little Sally Combes is caring too much for th
young newshound," Mrs Bernstein said to her husband
as they took their last walk round the deck before retir
ing to bed. "She is upset because he keeps his eyes and
nose to the scent instead of to her."

"Which scent, I wonder?" Max answered. "The
stewardess on the deck below us who goes ashore ver
smart, full of smiles and comes back exhausted, dejected
Who may perhaps have drowned Mrs Fennister in a f
of jealousy . . . ?"

"That is what I meant," Lottie Bernstein answered
"Have you other scents our hound could be following?"

"Two, I think," Max told her calmly. "It is not such
simple story as most of us are coming to believe. I to
thought it was jealousy; Mario and Conchita in love
Felicity desperate, suicide; or the lovers conspiring to ri
themselves of the wife. But nothing since that night reall
fits either of those conclusions, do you think?"

"Perhaps you are right," Lottie said. "You so ver
often are right, my dearest Max."

"Then I admit to myself a third possibility. The lover
conspire but they are forestalled. Felicity is beaten ur
concious and tipped overboard by someone who though
she knew too much."

"About what?"

Max shrugged impressively.

"I am not God to know every detail of every man's secrets."

"Then you are guessing."

"With reason, Lottie. Has it occurred to you, playing bridge, taking drinks in the lounge, watching their general behaviour, their clothes, her imitation jewellery, that Sir John and Lady Meadows are very, very short of money?"

Lottie sighed, shook her head at the persistent sorrows of mankind, but agreed.

"I think he went ashore at Bridgetown to borrow but was unsuccessful. I think they both went ashore today. Perhaps they succeeded, or a little, not enough."

"But why should they want to borrow during the voyage? They will have paid for the travel in England and they can take fifty pounds each with them. That should be enough while not going ashore."

"We are straying from my point. That Mrs Fennister may have been attacked because she knew too much about the Meadows pair, perhaps because she not only knew but was exacting blackmail."

"Oh no!" Mrs Bernstein was shocked. "I won't believe that. The Meadows with an unmentionable secret! A straightforward, so well-mannered, so very nearly stupid . . . pair . . . surely . . . !"

"My dear Lottie, you must not recite the characteristics of sixty years ago. Titled Englishmen have changed since then, with wars and impoverishment. We must not fall into the errors of the French who make stereotypes that they believe in and repeat for a hundred years and more. It is the Englishman of 1890, tweeds, rabbit teeth, wealth, that de Gaulle fears to let into E.E.C."

"This has nothing to do with Felicity Fennister," Lottie said severely. "I refuse to consider the Meadows. Who else would have wished to—to silence that poor girl?"

"Our dubious bridge players," Max told her. "Also I think they are much more likely to be criminals and poor Felicity may not have known that she held fatal knowledge of them. I would prefer to think her incapable of blackmail."

Lottie took his arm and smiled lovingly at him.

"You have, of course, no proof whatever of these wild theories."

"No," he answered, smiling back. "Nor shall I unless Sir John comes to borrow money from me or Tim Rogers is hit on the head and thrown overboard."

CHAPTER VIII

That night in port was unbearably hot. *Selena*'s air-conditioning was scarcely adequate and most of the passengers came to breakfast the next morning complaining of headaches and sleeplessness.

Among them Sally, whose wakeful hours had been caused less by the temperature than by the very confused state of her feelings about Tim. He, on the other hand, already at the table when she arrived, greeted her with cheerful unconcern and trivial conversation, excused himself the moment he had finished without asking about her plans for the day and was gone until the afternoon.

Sally's boredom and resentment grew. The wish to return to Bermuda and from there as quickly as possible to England came back to her with increased force. In fact she got as far as the top of the gangway prepared to go ashore and telephone a cable to her uncle, regardless of cost, when Ian and his wife came up to her.

"Are you booked for anything special?" Helen asked.

"I thought I'd do a bit of shopping," Sally lied, hoping to put off the pair.

"Splendid," Ian said, with his usual air of having arranged the universe to his satisfaction while giving personal attention to one small item in the pattern.

"You can join up with Helen who was binding at having to go alone. I've a date with the local butchery, you see."

"He means the hospital," Helen explained. "These surgeons!"

"I gathered that," Sally said coldly. But she was quite pleased to have Helen with her to go into the town and gradually as they walked away from the burning quayside her wish to get in touch with Bermuda faded and her eagerness to spend the money in her bag no longer included the price of a telephone call.

The two girls spent a happy morning choosing small presents for their distant families before making their slow way back to the ship for a necessary shower before lunch.

Tim had not come back. Or at any rate he was not present for lunch. Except for the rest of the medical contingent who had been to Maracas to bathe the day before and could not afford another expensive trip, the passengers were all away. All except Sir John and Lady Meadows, Sally noticed, who sat alone at the Captain's table, for he himself did not appear for this meal. Sally remembered that he very rarely did so.

Lunch over and nothing due to happen until they sailed again at dawn the next day Sally decided that a siesta was about the only way of passing some of the time pleasurably. Besides, a restless night, a long hot walk and an indifferent but filling lunch had made her sleepy. So she went dreamily to her cabin.

Conchita was there, crouched beside the bed under the windows, her head on her arms, sobbing wildly.

Sally's initial dismay and anger soon turned to pity at this very real distress. She hurried to Conchita's side, sat down on the bed and tried to make her lift her head.

"You've come back—again!" was all she found to say.

The stewardess's sobs had begun to lessen as soon as she heard the door of the cabin open. She had been prepared for an enemy, or at least someone totally unsympathetic. But after all it had been Miss Combes, a poor silly English girl, but basically kind, however ignorant of the ways of the world.

Conchita lifted her head at last, fumbling in the pocket of her uniform dress for a handkerchief.

"Now tell me," Sally said. "Only get up first, won't you, and sit beside me."

Conchita's eyes filled with tears again as Sally helped

her up and put an arm round her shoulders to encourage her.

"We thought you'd left the ship for good this time," Sally went on, uncertain whether this would promote confession or cause another collapse.

"I meant it so," Conchita said. "Oh, God, that he should not be here either! Not in Barbados, no word. Again in Trinidad, no word, no sign, nothing!"

"You are speaking of Mr Fennister, aren't you?" Sally asked.

Conchita nodded, wiping her eyes and blowing her nose. Sally waited.

"He promised to meet you in Bridgetown? You—you were having an affair with him?"

Conchita's swollen, reddened eyes, grew angry.

"An affair! Holy Virgin, I am his wife!"

So she acknowledged it. Tim had not made up his tale of the marriage, or had he?

"I knew that really," Sally told her. "I just wanted you to tell me yourself."

Conchita nodded again.

"That rat of an Englishman! That snooping devil! I knew he would betray me! I knew—"

It was Sally's turn to become angry.

"Why should he not tell me? Why should you or Mario for that matter—want to hide it?"

"Because that partner of his—that sly little wire-walker—she called herself Mrs Fennister. Fennister! He is Mario Fenestri and I am Conchita Fenestri. She had no right—"

"Perhaps she was not to blame. Have you tried to find out if he really married her—legally, I mean? I know it wouldn't be legal, it would be bigamy. But he may have thought you were dead."

Conchita hung her head at this.

"Why did you leave him?" Sally asked, relentless now that Conchita was willing to talk.

"Because he wanted—he insisted—to go to Europe.

And I was afraid. I was a dancer—good, you know, but not of the first rank. He was an acrobat, good too, but again not of the first rank."

"But I thought he was famous!" Sally interrupted.

"His act is famous. That woman made it so. It was her act that held the audience. He supported her. That was all."

"So now?"

"So now the act is dead."

She said this with such dark malignancy in her voice that Sally shrank away from her.

"You should have gone with him to Europe," she stammered. She had to learn the rest of the story but she dreaded the end of it, even though she thought she knew it all.

"I was afraid," Conchita told her. This seemed to be true enough, but Sally was still puzzled.

"Why?"

"Because our two acts were separate. And not first-class. Perhaps we may be engaged together, perhaps not. Perhaps we have to separate. Perhaps we do not make enough money. Perhaps we are too poor, and failed and not enough money to come back home. I was afraid."

"So Mario went to Europe alone. He had saved enough for this?"

"He had taken my savings to add to his own. He went away without telling. But I knew . . ."

This was not exactly how Tim had described the end of the marriage. In his account it was Conchita who had pulled out and Mario, deserted, who had then taken himself to Europe in a last desperate attempt to make his career. But Sally did not dispute what she had been told. She understood now, more clearly than ever, that one did not argue with Conchita.

There was silence between them for a time. Then Conchita sighed wearily, looked at her watch and prepared to get up and go.

"Wait," Sally said, seeing this fine opportunity about

to end. "You've told me about this terrible situation you and the Fennisters were in. But it's ended now, hasn't it? Was it Felicity's own doing, or yours, or his? You know, don't you? You must know. You were there—on the deck —all three of you, that night. You were seen by several people."

Conchita leaped to her feet. Her face, the powder streaked by tears, was a yellowish mask, except for the reddened eyes, the reddened nose. A clown's mask, Sally thought, on her own feet too. A clown's face, ludicrous and tragic.

"I am afraid!" Conchita cried. "He say he leave her or make her leave him. Yes, I see them together that night. I watch and he come away alone on that A deck. He is very sad. Very strange."

"Only *sad!*" Sally was profoundly shocked. "If he'd killed her he'd surely be more than *sad!*"

"You understand *nothing*." Conchita muttered, turning away. But before she reached the door she whipped round again. "That book he was reading. You give it back to the library. There was nothing in it. He insist she leave a note—suicide note, he said. In the book. I must find it and give to the police."

"Why leave it to you to do this?"

Conchita's face twisted in pain.

"Because he might not be believed. Because he would not say I was his true wife. I was to find the note as stewardess. No one would be given his cabin."

"But I was given it," Sally said. "I wonder why that was done?"

"I am afraid," Conchita said monotonously. It was like a litany, Sally thought, this repeated confession of weakness but without any added prayer for mercy. She turned again to go. This time she did not stop but went out of the cabin closing the door gently behind her.

Sally double locked it at once, then transferred the suicide note to her handbag. She had at last decided to give it to Captain Crowthorne and was sorry she had not done so before. Her talk with Conchita, who had undoubtedly been searching for it again without success, had made some things clear. The stewardess had indeed been married to Mario Fenestri. Tim was right in that. So Felicity was the interloper. In Conchita's simple primitive passionate soul there was only one wish, one problem. To remove Felicity. Mario knew she was capable of doing this herself. He had to forestall her. How? He certainly did not want to destroy the new, successful act. He probably did not want to live with Conchita again. So a planted note, to be written by Felicity and she would get ashore early to wait for him. He would give Conchita the note, or tell her where to find it, say Felicity must have thrown herself overboard, join her in Bermuda and fly off to South America as planned.

But why then the scene on A deck, Felicity's undoubted disappearance from it, this disappearance advertised and all that had followed? Had the plan gone wrong? Had another, more ruthless, more truly criminal character intervened because Felicity knew or recognised or was in some way dangerous to another passenger?

This simple reasoning brought Sally to the point Max Bernstein had reached the day before and with as little satisfaction. Except that it increased her determination to hand over the only real piece of evidence, true or false in content, a forgery or otherwise, that had been found.

Sally took off her shirt and slacks and lay down on her bunk, to follow her programme in spite of the highly emotional interlude with Conchita which had obviously put paid to any hope of sleep.

She was wrong, however. She began to drowse as soon as she had stretched out on the bunk. In four minutes she was asleep and did not move again until half past four when she woke sweating, with a dry mouth and a headache.

A shower improved matters. A cup of tea would complete the cure. Dressed, her hair brushed and her make-up renewed Sally wandered along to the lounge.

The first person she saw was Tim, sitting in a corner with a tray in front of him holding two cups and a notebook beside it in which he was writing busily. He looked up as she went in and waved to her. She waved back but she had caught another signal from the middle of the room, so she obeyed this instead, much to Tim's annoyance.

Mrs Longford said as Sally sat down at her table, "I do envy you young things. A whole day and a half in port and you look as fresh as a rose bud. How d'you do it?"

Mrs Longford, in pale green linen, looked the picture of cool good looks herself, Sally thought, but she said, smiling, "Just a siesta and a shower. I shopped this morning so there was nothing else to do."

"Which is the object of the exercise—of the cruise, I mean," Mrs Longford said, handing Sally a cup of tea. "Ah, here comes the steward. Have a cress sandwich."

"Do they grow cress in Trinidad?" Sally asked.

"I shouldn't think so."

As the steward waited for them to choose cakes or biscuits Mrs Longford asked him. "You ought to know where the cooks get cress. They grow it on the blankets we don't need in the tropics, don't they?"

The man grinned and wheeled his trolley away.

"I wouldn't be surprised if they actually did," Mrs Longford said.

Sally said nothing. She sipped her tea and ate her cress sandwich and avoided catching Tim's eye when she looked up. She wondered why Mrs Longford wanted to talk to her and how long it would be before she stopped her very feeble flattery and still wetter jokes and came to the point.

This was reached when Mrs Longford finished her second cup of tea. She said, "Are you busy, Sally? But of course you're not. I want a little talk with you. About Conchita, actually. You had quite a session with her after lunch, didn't you? No, wait till we get by ourselves. No, I mean that."

The voice had become uncommonly sharp, even commanding. Sally's instinct was to rebel against such unwarranted authority, such interference, but her curiosity won. So she followed the older woman meekly enough, still avoiding Tim's eyes which she felt were upon her and her companion as they stepped out on to the deck and proceeded slowly forward on the side away from the shore.

"Have you too been talking to Conchita?" Sally asked. She was determined to break Mrs Longford's initiative.

"Yes, Sally. That woman is desperate and I think dangerous. She insists she is Mario's wife—"

"She *is* Mario's wife," Sally interrupted. "She told Tim about his desertion and the way she had followed him. He verified this story afterwards."

"But not the fact that *she* deserted *him*."

Sally did not answer this. Of course Mrs Longford had it from Felicity, if not from Mario himself. Whichever way round it was Mario had gone to Europe alone and had married Felicity, though he had no proof he was free to do so. In fact he was not free. None of it altered the fact that Conchita was the one to search and pursue, not Mario. And the marriage was not destroyed. There had not and could not have been a divorce, since both were Roman Catholics.

"She deserted him," Mrs Longford went on, "after he insisted upon trying his luck in Europe and she refused to leave South America. When he had found work in Germany he went back to get her but she had disappeared."

"He was only twenty-four when he married her. There were no children. They were together only three years. I don't think he tried very hard to find her when he went back. He was afraid of spoiling his chances in Germany, which he had worked so hard for. He was thirty-one when he met Felicity. She'd been mad on gym at school, nearly up to Olympic standards—especially vaulting and balance and so on. She was with a small English troupe in Hamburg and Mario was with a Spanish set of acrobats in the same circus. They met and fell in love and worked out an act for the two of them that was so sensational they put it into a combined effort of the two teams. After that agents' offers came pouring in. They were married two months later. Mario told me all about his former marriage, only he implied that Conchita was dead."

"So when she turned up on the boat as a stewardess he had to tell her she was very much alive?"

Mrs Longford nodded, a disdainful look on her face.

"Was Mrs Fennister—Felicity—very much upset?"

"Naturally."

"To the point of committing suicide? I mean," Sally said desperately as Mrs Longford turned away, "I mean didn't Captain Crowthorne show you the note I found? To verify her writing? He said he would and had. He wanted to keep it—"

"But you wouldn't give it to him. He told me about it. How could I verify the writing when you kept the thing?"

"Conchita thinks there was a note. She wants to prove it was suicide because she's afraid Mario did it."

"Did what?"

"Pushed Felicity overboard. Conchita thinks she saw him do it. She almost told me so. It was what she meant."

"Unless she did it herself. The note would be equally good cover for her own act—if she did it."

Sally became suddenly obstinate.

"I don't believe it was either of them. Mario would never have destroyed the act. It had cost him too much to make it. Conchita wouldn't have the strength—the physical strength—to get a trained and highly skilled acrobat over the rail, someone much younger than herself, very much stronger in every way. Unless she was unconscious and I don't see Conchita working that one

93

out. She hasn't much brain, has she?"

"So you would plump for suicide, would you?" Mrs Longford said, looking at Sally, curiously intent upon her answer.

The girl did not care for the look. She remembered Tim's hints about the other dubious passengers. She remembered Mrs Longford's apparent indifference, her callous indifference, to Felicity's loss. Had the girl known something also known only to Mrs Longford, perhaps involving Mrs Longford—?

On a sudden impulse Sally opened her handbag and took out the note.

"Here it is," she said, handing it over. "Now. Is that your sister's writing or isn't it?"

If Mrs Longford was pleased she did not show it. If she was triumphant, having worked so hard for this result, it could not be read in her face as she held the bit of paper between finger and thumb, staring at it. At last she said, "Yes, this is Felicity's writing. The paper looks like half a sheet of the ship's note paper, the half without the heading. But it proves nothing, does it? Beyond the fact that my sister put the words on the paper. So," and she lifted cold eyes to Sally's face, "it is of no value to any of us and perhaps a danger to you. Don't you think so?"

"I think I will give it to Captain Crowthorne," Sally said.

"Oh, I don't think that's necessary," Mrs Longford answered.

Quite slowly she tore the note across and across again until it was reduced to quite small pieces. Then she dropped them into the harbour. A rush of gulls swooped down and rose disappointed. A number of slim dark shapes rose from the depths, sucked a few pieces under and disappeared. Mrs Longford, brushing her hands together, nodded at Sally with a little smile and walked away.

94

CHAPTER IX

Selena left Port of Spain early the next morning, sailing north-west towards the rocky islands of the Serpent's Mouth, or Dragon's Teeth as they are variously called, and the not far distant mountainous shores of Venezuela.

Sally made no effort this time to get up to watch their start. She heard the various movements and orders, ringing bells, tramping feet, churning waters, but she merely turned on her side and let herself slip back into the untroubled sleep these things had disturbed.

Not so Tim Rogers. He was up very early indeed; he had in fact not gone to bed at all, but had spent the night checking the various movements of those passengers whose arrivals or returning presences interested him. When the lounge was empty, its lights dimmed, its doors on to the deck locked, he retreated to his cabin on C deck for a time and lay on his bunk entering these interesting items in his notebook. Later he got up again to prowl about as before, noticed only by the crew on watch, who never paid much attention to that herd of wealthy pigs, as they regarded them, who paid so much to be transported in idleness to the discomforts of an alien climate, strange shores, after uncomfortable sick-making travel to reach them.

Tim was on B deck when the tugs arrived to move *Selena* from her berth at the quayside. She had no room to go ahead or astern as she lay, so she had first to have her head swung out a little, then her stern, then her head again until by degrees the pulling and pushing cleared her enough to allow her to be swung on to her course and begin to proceed under her own power. It was, as always, a fascinating manoeuvre to watch. Tim was enthralled by it, and did not notice until it was over that several of the passengers were beside him, all watching, among them Mr Newbuckle and Sir John Meadows.

"So you've joined us again, Rogers," Sir John said in a friendly voice.

"With a load of stories for his editor, I'll be bound. Eh, lad?" Mr Newbuckle followed, without giving Tim time to answer.

"Well, yes," the journalist said, hoping to satisfy both. He added, to guide the conversation away from his own doings, "Wonderful sight, isn't it, seeing a ship moved about without bumping anything at all. When you think of the tonnage and the fact she's on a moving surface . . ."

"And then think how often your car's bashed by clots parked fore and aft that you haven't even squeezed!"

Mr Newbuckle laughed at Sir John's complaint. Tim said, "I must just see if all the tugs have left us," and walked away to the other side of the deck. What he really wanted to check was whether the bridge players had made an early morning appearance. They had come aboard at the last possible moment the night before, since the gangway had been raised in readiness for the dawn start. Or was it to prevent late visitors, invited or uninvited? Unwanted, at any rate.

He was disappointed. The bridge players were not on deck. So they would be in their cabins on A deck, two doubles side by side. So he would not be able to look round in those cabins as he had hoped. Which was a pity, as he had managed to get keys made in Port of Spain from the impressions he had taken of the A deck steward's master keys. Expensive too and the account had already gone way up above the limit his paper had given him.

It was a hot day on the calm waters of the Caribbean as they proceeded on their way to the distant Bahamas and from there to Bermuda. This was to be their last port of call before returning to England. The passengers, after their activities on shore, lay about in deck chairs, wearing a minimum of clothing, with frequent visits to the swimming pool, whose tepid waters, heated by the sun and the hot bodies immersed in them, grew warmer still as the hours passed. No one tried to play a deck game, not even the gentle bowls, while the crew, stripped to the waist as usual, wore floppy straw hats and stood about in the shade of deck fixtures holding cleaning rags in their hands and doing nothing with them.

No one had much appetite for dinner that evening. Sally, who had noticed Tim sitting up at the bar next to Sir John Meadows, tried to catch his eye as she passed him, but meeting with no response went on to find Helen. The bossy Ian was still dressing, his wife said.

"He takes ages—always. I tell him if he's as slow operating as he is getting into his clothes his patients will all die of prolonged shock."

Sally laughed, pretty sure Helen would never dare to say any such thing. The poor woman must be really downtrodden, she reflected, to have to invent these fantasy rockets.

The general move down to the dining saloon was slow, ordering was unenthusiastic, in spite of the stewards pointing out some fresh dishes acquired in Port of Spain. Tim, especially, hardly ate at all and spoke not a word. Sally noticed this and saw too that his usually healthy tan seemed to have faded to a strange, greenish yellow. When finally he got up without excusing himself, to totter away with a steward at his elbow, the Chief Officer said, "Seasick! Well, I'll be—"

Sally said, "More likely the heat. It's been pretty frightful today! Anyway, he's been off the ship since Barbados. Lost his immunity or whatever it is."

The newcomers at the table, taking the places of the missionaries and teachers, were Trinidadians bound for England to visit relations and return on the next cruise. They had been introduced to Tim but knew nothing about him. Neither Sally nor the Chief Officer felt inclined to explain. The Chief Officer began a new conversation about Trinidad, while Sally finished her own meal in silence.

As soon as she left the table she began to worry about Tim. He was certainly ill and she remembered an early boast he had made of being a very good sailor. If someone as liable to be upset as herself felt perfectly well then Tim was not seasick. But he was ill. So what kind of illness? Something he had eaten on shore? Something infectious he had caught on shore—or on the plane— in Bridgetown or Port of Spain?

Would he have called for his cabin steward? Could she go to his cabin and find out? She didn't even know the number on C deck. She felt unwilling to ask, but she couldn't go knocking at all the doors until he answered.

Mrs Fairbrother was in her usual place in the lounge when Sally arrived there. She was sympathetic.

"You can always tell the cabin steward you are anxious," she said. "That wouldn't be misunderstood. Let him go and find out."

While she was still uncertain how to act, half inclined to leave matters as they were since Tim had given so many recent hints of his lack of interest in herself, the stewards came in to fix a screen for a film show. The listless passengers welcomed their arrival with clapping.

Sally watched the two ancient flickering pictures with genuine simple amusement and found when she next looked at her watch that the time was eleven o'clock and that most of the older passengers had melted away.

All her anxiety came flooding back with a new quite unreasonable feeling of guilt. She hurried away from the lounge and while still uncertain how to find her way to Tim's cabin without embarrassment wandered about on the decks taking the usual constitutional round A deck from the lounge double doors, down to B deck near the swimming pool and then down to the foredeck where she had watched the flying fish on her first day out.

She found Tim right up in the bows where passengers were not supposed to go. He was sprawled beside a coil

98

of heavy rope, his head and shoulders supported on it, his arms flung wide, his face ghastly in the dim glow of the ship's lights.

She cried "Tim!" as she flung herself down beside him. "Tim, darling. I've been looking everywhere for you!"

This was so untrue, so inadequate, so shaming, that she burst into bitter tears.

The tears seemed to rouse him. He struggled into a half-sitting position, leaning on one elbow and groaning.

"Sick!" he managed to gasp. "No—not seasick—poisoned!"

He began to retch again. Obviously he couldn't walk, but he must be got below to his bunk. To a doctor.

"I'll get help," Sally said, scrambling to her feet. As she did so she came up against a figure standing just behind her. It was Dick Groves, his white uniform ghostly in the pale light.

Tim collapsed again. Sally explained quickly.

"I'll get help," she cried, forgetting Dick was an officer if only a cadet and could easily find the ship's doctor, the most suitable person to come to the rescue.

But Sally was away, running to the iron staircase that led right up to the bridge, with openings on each deck on the way. As she climbed she remembered Tim had gasped 'Poison'. She remembered Dick had muttered 'Doc, yes, at once' before she had forestalled him by darting off. Always making the wrong move! Silly twit! She climbed, blaming herself, desperately afraid for Tim, totally confused.

Because how was *she* to find Dr McRae? Fool that she was not to let Dick do his stuff. He was trained for it, wasn't he? Whereas she—

She found herself stumbling on to the bridge. The large figure of Captain Crowthorne strode towards her, behind him a woman was moving quickly away and in two seconds had disappeared. Mrs Longford, she thought, suddenly inclined to break into bawdy laughter. She choked, stammered out her news, was pushed gently away from the bridge and held by her arm while the Captain gave a few brief orders.

"Now, Miss Combes, you had better go straight to your cabin. You're very upset, I can see. I'll send the stewardess to you."

"Conchita!" Sally cried. "No, you don't! Tim's poisoned and it may be that woman did it!"

Sally twisted her arm loose from his grasp and clattered away down the steep iron staircase, down to the deck where she found Dick had been joined by two seamen and the doctor himself, all of them busily preparing to lift Tim on to a stretcher. Quick work. Her silly panic had done nothing but annoy Captain Crowthorne, interrupting his philandering—it could not be more serious than that—not openly on his bridge with other officers around.

She heard Tim's faint voice, speaking her name.

"I'm here," she said clearly, her heart torn by the pain in his twisted face and sunken eyes.

"Closer."

She knelt by the stretcher. Dr McRae stooped to say, "If we don't get him in at once and treat him we'll most likely lose him."

But Tim's eyes compelled her attention.

"Quick, Tim," she whispered. "One word . . ."

It was no good. The retching began again. He tried to catch at her hand but the seamen at either end of the stretcher heaved it up and moved rapidly away with it, the doctor forced to trot to keep up with them.

Dick put an arm round Sally who was now crying again, openly and unashamedly.

"Not to worry too badly," he soothed. "I bet he's brought up most of what seems to have disagreed with him."

"Disagreed! You—you nut, don't you realise he's been poisoned! Deliberately!"

Dick had not realised. Indeed he did not believe it. He

simply thought the girl was raving. But he was afraid of aggravating her hysteria. So he said, very quickly and quietly, "And who would think of doing such a thing? And why?"

Sally shook her head. She was beginning to feel that there was something dark and sinister about all that happened on this ship, about most of the passengers, certainly about the officers.

How was it that Dr McRae arrived before she had time to return from the bridge? Dick could have been on watch and chanced upon her and Tim. But weren't they out of sight at deck level? But perhaps not from the bridge? Then had Captain Crowthorne seen Tim or at any rate watched her find him and sent at once for the doctor, the sailors, even Dick?

She looked up at him. A hard look, he noticed, nothing hysterical about it.

"He was deliberately poisoned," she said slowly, "because he knows things some people want kept hidden. He'll have to be protected."

Dick found himself stammering, "How about you, then? If Rogers knows things and you know he does, won't you be a target too?"

"As if that mattered!" she cried, with a gesture she meant to be dismissive but which Dick, a little bemused again, found pathetically noble.

When she turned and began to walk away he followed her, so they arrived together outside Tim's cabin and were together there, waiting, when Dr McRae came out, followed by Ian and his wife Helen.

"He'll do," Dr McRae said, looking at Sally. "He got rid of most of it, I think, and perhaps in any case not a lethal dose for his age and size. Shock will be the main trouble and dehydration. Our surgical colleague here has put up a drip. Our medical colleagues are taking the next watch. You look as if a sedative wouldn't come amiss for you, young woman."

"Can I see him?" Sally asked.

"Just now, no. Last thing he'd want and I forbid it. To bed wi' ye, lassie. In the morn, maybe."

His relapse into his native form of speech surprised him as much as it did Sally. He realised he had been quite rattled by this case. He had none of Dick Groves' reservations. He had met poison cases before on board, though not so far among the passengers. With a very mixed crew of several nationalities, some hot-tempered and from countries where a great variety of noxious herbs grew freely, he had for many years carried a generous supply of suitable antidotes and also a primitive but reasonably useful set of appropriate tests.

Having seen Sally to her cabin and despatched Dick with a brief scribbled note, sealed, for the Captain, he went to his own cabin and in the small locked annexe to it, that served both as dispensary and lab, he applied his chosen tests to the specimens he had collected and found them positive. He had already begun the correct treatment, so he rang for the steward and ordered coffee and a sandwich. Two-hourly visits to the patient for the next twelve hours and if all went well young Rogers would then be on the mend. The junior auxiliaries were a great comfort. Good for them, too. They were going to spend a year in Jamaica in their various specialities. Good experience for them, this poisoning. And lucky for him it had happened when it did and not after they left the Bahamas. He was too old to sit up at attention all night long.

When the steward came with the coffee, Dr McRae told him to rouse him in two hours' time and repeat that until he went off duty. When the steward had gone he got out a bottle of rum and added a generous tot to the coffee. It was routine with him by now. It worked very well.

Sally was not allowed to see Tim for two days. She fretted, but knew it was sense to obey orders. Besides, the young doctors who were really nursing and treating the case under Dr McRae's orders told her all about it.

Probably a concoction of the seeds of one of the oleanders, having an irritant effect very similar to arsenic. Possibly arsenic itself. Easy to come by if you knew the ropes.

Armed with this knowledge she did not waste any of the precious ten minutes allowed her for a visit to Tim.

"They'll have told you what it was," he forestalled her. "Ian and Co, I mean. The old boy could have got hold of it all right. He went ashore at Bridgetown."

"Who?" she asked, puzzled.

"Not that I stayed there on that account. No, something much more interesting. Did you think I'd gone without saying a word?"

"I wondered."

"Were you riled? I bet you were. Did you start up something with Dick Groves?"

"Idiot!" She felt her cheeks burning. "Vain, smart-alec, needling devil!"

He put an arm up round her neck and pulled.

"Kiss me," he ordered.

When the ten minutes were up, Helen looked in and said, "Interview over."

"One minute," Tim begged. Helen retreated.

"Listen," he said. "Something you must look out for. On no account accept a drink or anything else from old Meadows."

"Sir John? Why ever not?"

"Because it was he tried to put me under. I saw him switch his drink for mine. We were up at the bar before dinner."

"I know. You wouldn't look at me."

"I was waiting for my gin and tonic. He'd ordered one too. It came. He spoke to me, asked me to join him and his wife. Pointed her out. I turned to look. When I turned back I noticed he'd picked up my drink and left his for me."

"Why didn't you say?"

"Because they were both gins."

"The minute's up," Helen said from the doorway.

CHAPTER X

Bundled out of Tim's cabin by Helen's orders, reinforced by Helen's hands, Sally went first of all to her own cabin to recover. She was confused, totally overthrown by the sight of her darling Tim so weak and drawn. Also considerably annoyed by Helen's bossy manner. Worse than Ian, she thought, in an upsurge of plain fury. Women doctors! Then remembering how meek Helen was when Ian threw his weight about, she could not help laughing in spite of her over-all distress. Helen getting her own back, poor drip. Well, let her try. But she'd put her money on Ian every time, damn him! Damn them both for keeping her away from her love.

That Tim was indeed her love she had now no doubt at all. As far as she was concerned this was the real thing —at last. Different from any sort of feeling she had experienced before with a mild succession of boy-friends since she was—well—seventeen. It did not occur to her that at twenty-three, getting on for middle-age, she was still susceptible to change. She was sure of herself and today she had felt sure of Tim.

When she had recovered from her inner turmoil sufficiently to present a calm appearance to the world, Sally went in search of Mrs Fairbrother. Her elderly friend was not in her usual place on deck nor in any other part of it, but Sally found her at last in the library, where the girl had gone in the end to write a letter to her mother, having neglected this duty for more than a week.

Mrs Fairbrother was hidden behind the note-paper rack on the last table. She leaned from her place when she saw Sally and whispered, "Letter writing, my dear? Come and have tea with me when you've finished. In my cabin.

I'll order it. We can't talk in the lounge and I know you have a great many things to tell me."

She disappeared again and Sally sat down, relieved to find her path to confidence and confession made so easy and so pleasant. Her letter home was filled with a description of Port of Spain, the drive to Maracas, the tropical vegetation, the interesting mixed population. Not a word about Tim, not a hint of drama.

Mrs Fairbrother's spacious cabin on A deck, with tea prepared and waiting for her, completed Sally's cure. She was able to describe in detail how she had found Tim desperately ill, how she had panicked and rushed up to the bridge and how Captain Crowthorne had dealt with the whole situation.

"I admire that man," Mrs Fairbrother said when the girl had finished her story. "Events never seem to catch him out. You must be right, quite right. Either he or his officers actually saw what had happened to Tim or it was reported to him. After all," she added reflectively, "though we hardly ever see them, there must be quite a large number of men running this ship. In the engine room alone, not to mention the deck work. And then the catering and all that—"

Sally broke in on Mrs Fairbrother's catalogue.

"Tim says Sir John Meadows switched drinks with him and so must have given him the poison."

"Nonsense!" Mrs Fairbrother was shocked. "Complete nonsense! What could possibly make him think that?"

"Because he was sitting up to the bar next to Tim. Because he deliberately took Tim's attention off their glasses. They were both having gin and tonic. Sir John must have heard Tim order earlier and asked for the same."

"If they were the same how does he know they were switched, as you call it? Did it taste different? Was the level in the glass different?"

"I don't know."

In fact Sally knew nothing beyond the fact that Tim had warned her to avoid Sir John because he believed the latter had tried to get rid of him.

"There'd be no possible motive," Mrs Fairbrother said firmly. "I thought we'd discarded the idea that Felicity was got rid of because she knew things. I still believe Conchita was at the bottom of it, perhaps in league with Mario."

Sally shook her head.

"I don't agree. Conchita is afraid for Mario. She isn't afraid for herself, only for him."

Mrs Fairbrother shrugged and poured out second cups of tea for them both.

"If we discard Conchita," she said between sips, "we must find someone else, another urgent need to stop Tim's too clever probing, another secret to be kept. I refuse to consider Sir John. But what about those men who nearly always win at bridge and try to raise the stakes while they play?"

"I don't agree to discard Sir John. Tim said—"

"I still refuse to consider Sir John. I don't care what Tim said."

There was a pause. Mrs Fairbrother looked stern. Sally tried again.

"What about Mr Bernstein then?"

"You shock me, Sally. Ex-refugees, with their appalling history?"

This was sheer sentimentality, Sally decided, but did not say so.

"Besides," Mrs Fairbrother went on, "they're rolling, Lady Meadows told me. But of course she may have been wrong."

"I expect she was right," Sally answered. "How about the Newbuckles? They're pretty well rolling too, aren't they?"

Mrs Fairbrother laughed so heartily that Sally, who had not been trying to be funny, had to join in.

"We won't go any further north," Mrs Fairbrother said.

"I'm sure they're all as honest as the day. We must look for our villains—or villainesses—in the south. In the tropics, as I said at the beginning. I still believe this whole nasty business is really a simple story."

"Why not Mrs Longford?" Sally asked, still unwilling to bring their speculations back to Conchita and the absent Mario.

"Yes." Mrs Fairbrother was instantly serious. "You actually saw her, late at night, on the bridge with the Captain?"

"It was a woman I thought I recognised as Mrs Longford, but I didn't see her at all well," Sally answered thoughtfully. "Of course as she's a friend of his there's no reason why he shouldn't ask her up there to look at the instruments and that sort of thing. He wasn't alone. There were at least two other men in uniform. I hadn't time to see which."

"That's all very well," Mrs Fairbrother told her. "But you don't mean it. What you really thought was you'd run in on Captain Crowthorne necking, or snogging don't you young people call it these days, and he got rid of her and put you out in a couple of seconds flat?"

Sally laughed again.

"Could be," she said.

Later that day she tried to see Tim again but was told he was much better and sleeping. On her way up to her own cabin she passed Conchita going down.

The stewardess stopped abruptly.

"Mr Rogers—poor boy—he recovers?" she asked, in a whisper.

"Come to my cabin," Sally said on a sudden impulse.

"Ten minutes, I come," the stewardess answered.

It was half an hour before Conchita knocked at Sally's cabin door. The girl, who had double-locked it, let her in and made her sit on the unused bunk under the windows. It was growing dark outside. With the top light on in the cabin they were both visible from the deck, so Sally pulled the curtains together before seating herself on her own bed.

"Mr Rogers is quite well again," she said. "But he has been very ill, as I'm sure you know. Everyone on board this ship who knew him earlier thinks he was poisoned—deliberately."

Conchita nodded, a grave, dignified nod, not in the least afraid, not conceivably guilty.

"Who did that wicked thing?" Sally asked, fiercely.

Conchita shook her head.

"I speak to no one. They do not speak to me. They say to themselves I do it. But how I do it? I am not in the kitchens or the steward's pantry to put something in one man's dish."

"I think it may have been in a drink."

"A drink with the dinner?"

"A drink before the dinner. In the lounge bar."

Again Conchita shook her head, her dark eyes dull, her smooth, olive-coloured face calm.

"Then you can tell me nothing?" Sally asked, growing impatient. "We have these mysteries, these murderous attacks, not fatal this time, thank God, but too nearly so and you say you know nothing. Very well, you had better go, then. It is nearly dinner time and I must dress."

But a change had come over Conchita while she listened to the angry voice. She got up, spread her arms, then brought her hands together and clasped them close to her body.

"Not this, not Mr Rogers," she cried in a stricken voice. "Of this I know nothing. But that girl, my Mario's girl, she who falsely used my name, Mrs Fennister, curses upon her . . . Oh, blessed Mary, mother of God . . . !"

"What about Mrs Fennister? Tell me. Tell me!"

Sally jumped up, seizing Conchita by the shoulders and shaking her violently until her head began to fall backwards and forwards. To her intense inward astonishment the woman made no attempt to fight back or even to release herself. Sally let her go

108

"Tell me!" she repeated. "Or shall I fetch the Captain and he will order you to speak."

It was a silly, empty threat, but it broke the last of Conchita's resistance. She said stonily, "Mario, my husband, is a murderer. I saw it, I saw him throw that partner, that lying Felicity, over the rail into the sea."

So she had actually seen it done, Sally thought, watching the woman collapse on to the bed again, covering her face with her hands, her shoulders heaving.

Whether the appalling act had been of her prompting, her conniving, or merely the result of unrelenting pressure did not matter now. She had spoken with a certainty that must mean the plain truth of the event. So she was an accessory, certainly after, probably before as well. This was a confession of a kind but too vague. Also before only one witness, though a disinterested one.

"Tell me what you saw, Conchita. Tell me exactly what you know."

"Many times I spoke to Mario. I demanded he say I am his wife. I cannot wait. From Bermuda they go by air to Brazilia, first stop on their tour. I have no money to go with them. If I lose Mario again I will never, never find him. So I speak to him the last time. If he refuse I will claim him in the lounge before all the passengers. All peoples on this ship will know I am the wife, she is not. I make no objection to have her with us. I am not that much jealous as a woman. But he deny me and that is an insult. I will not have an insult."

She brooded upon the insult until Sally prompted her to go on with her story.

"So. He say he will explain, but she may not understand. She may wish to expose him equally with me. You understand?"

"Poor bloody nit!" Sally could not help exclaiming. It was wrong to treat this tragic tale so flippantly, but at that moment she was very near to laughter.

"It was a choice," Conchita answered grimly. "By all the blessed saints, it was a choice to make a man tremble."

"That was the night before the ship was due in at Bermuda? Go on."

"I watched when I could. I have heard since from others who were there that the two of them were making jokes, laughing, at dinner. Mario—making jokes—with his mind made up. For they had been shut in this cabin together for three hours before. Three hours. I know this. I have been told. It is the truth."

"And after dinner?" Sally was impatient. Time was passing and she began to be afraid there was not much genuine substance in Conchita's story. Too many other witnesses. Hearsay, didn't the lawyers call it? Not evidence.

"I watched them go to the lounge. Later I watched them come out. She went below. I approached him. He said, 'I am ready. I have decided what I shall do. You must not betray me.' Then I saw her coming back. He said, 'Wait here. Afterwards I will speak to you again.'"

"This was on A deck outside the lounge?" Sally asked.

"Yes. They walked away together. It was difficult to walk straight that night. I am used to the movement. They were professional at balance, you understand, but they swayed and moved from side to side as they walked. Even I moved away from the side to avoid spray."

"D'you mean the spray came up as high as A deck?"

"A little—yes. On B deck very wet. No one on A deck outside except those two."

Sally thought of Mrs Fairbrother's eavesdropping the Meadows pair and the Bernsteins. Sir John and Max had not been put off their respective late night strolls. But she only nodded to Conchita who went on with her tale.

"This now is what I saw. There was an argument again. I hear nothing for the noise of the sea and the wind. But I see him threaten her. I see her strike at his face. I see them close together, arms about each other, struggling. Then—ah—dear Lord, forgive me—I saw him pick her up above the rail and throw her outwards. Down, down into that raging sea!"

Conchita spoke the last of her description in Spanish, but accompanied it with such potent mime that Sally had no difficulty in understanding the full horror of her words. She sat on her bunk as frozen as the stewardess opposite.

At last she forced herself to say, "Then you spoke to him? Did you go to him or did he go to you?"

"He came to me. He said, 'She has jumped into the sea. Suicide. We will not speak together again on the ship. I will have to leave at Bermuda and I must arrange my affairs there, you understand. Then I will fly to Barbados and you will meet me there.'"

"So that was why you gave up your job on board?"

"He was not there." Conchita drew a deep breath.

Sally was puzzled.

"Are you sure? I mean, the ship was there for such a short time. I saw you leave and then you were back all in a rush. Perhaps he was late. Perhaps you got the meeting place wrong."

Conchita rose stiffly. Her face was a bitter tragic mask, very pale, Sally noticed, as she had been when she found her crying in the cabin.

"I am sure he double-cross me. I suspect it then. But I tell myself I have made a mistake. He has intended Port of Spain. I go ashore there. The same thing. I think he stay in Bermuda. But when we arrive there he will be gone. Murderer! Liar!"

Sally went to her. The woman's voice had risen; she was near to hysteria.

"Conchita! Stop it! Listen! Why did you ransack my cabin directly we got away from Bermuda? Were you looking for the suicide note? That was what you wanted to find, wasn't it? Well, I'm going to tell you something. There *was* such a note and it *was* hidden in a library book, a ship's library book. I took the book back and I kept the note."

Conchita shook her head sadly.

"I wanted it to prove the suicide."

111

"How did you know she'd written it? Because it *was* in her handwriting. Her real true handwriting."

"He say she told him there was a note. While he struggled to hold her. Or to throw her."

"You wanted to save him if he was suspected."

Conchita bowed her head in agreement.

"But now you don't. He's let you down and you've told me this story. And I can't disprove it. No one can. Because I no longer have this note, though the Chief Steward and the Purser and the Captain have all seen it and wanted to keep it for me. Or perhaps to destroy it."

Conchita's voice was sharp with fear.

"Why do you not have it any more? It may be I need it too."

"That's too bad, isn't it? But it's not my worry. Not any more. I'll tell you. I haven't got it because I showed it to Mrs Longford and she took it from me to read it and then she tore it up and threw the pieces into the sea."

Conchita swayed on her feet, gave a little choking cry and collapsed into a crumpled heap on the floor.

CHAPTER XI

Selena put into Kingston, Jamaica, for a few hours on the day Tim Rogers was pronounced out of danger. Captain Crowthorne had slowed his ship to decrease her movement during the first twenty-four hours after the attempt to kill the journalist. Also because he had his own investigations to make, interviews with his crew, with the catering staff; reports from the bar steward, the Chief Steward in the dining saloon; a report from Dr McRae on his tests, for which he had demanded and been given an even keel.

There was no doubt whatever about the poison. It could not have got into Tim's food or drink accidentally. But neither could it be proved which of these had been contaminated. Tim had kept his suspicions to himself and had made Sally promise not to repeat them. To her own astonishment she had kept this promise. It seemed a foolish thing to do but after all the Captain was not a police officer.

On the day *Selena* put into Kingston Tim went on deck again for the first time, walking slowly with Dr McRae's hand at his elbow and Sally following with two soft pillows.

"Not in sight of the snooper!" Tim exclaimed as they reached the shade near the swimming pool and saw Mrs Fairbrother start and her eyes brighten. He tried to turn back, ran into Sally, who was looking ahead, caught hold of her, felt a sudden access of strength, pulled her close, bent his head and kissed her hard.

"You'll do," Dr McRae said drily. "Take him away for'ard, Sally. I'll keep the good lady's attention from the pair of ye."

So for the rest of the morning Tim lay back on his pillows on a chaise-longue with his legs stretched out and Sally perched on a small hard chair beside him. She felt no discomfort until she got up to find her knees locked and her legs numb from the thigh down.

As soon as Tim was settled he took Sally's hand in his and did not let it go as they talked. Though the conversation was serious and seriously concentrated on their criminal problems, their hands made gentle love which they both welcomed, for it took them forward along a path each had begun to feel was as certain as it was desirable.

Sally described her second interview with Conchita.

"So she really does believe she saw Mario murdering Felicity. But she is so frightened for him she wanted to get hold of the suicide note. She fainted right off when I told her Mrs Longford destroyed it."

"I wonder why," Tim murmured.

"Why Mrs L tore it up or why Conchita collapsed?"

"Either. Both."

"Conchita because she'd lost an ace card."

"The Longford for the same reason, perhaps."

Sally shook her head.

"I simply don't understand Mrs Longford. She hasn't once behaved as if she felt any grief for her sister's death. She may not have any. She may have disapproved of her getting up her high-wire act with Mario or being an acrobat at all for that matter. I gather from Mrs Fairbrother Felicity was a good deal younger than Mrs L."

"But you don't suggest it was Mrs Longford who put Felicity over the rail?"

"Of course not. Conchita swears she saw—"

"We mustn't forget," Tim said slowly, "that Conchita married Mario in Brazil nine years ago, that he seems to have lost her two years later and married Felicity in London four years after that. He must be thirty-two or three now and Conchita a couple of years older."

"We know all that," Sally said frowning. "The point is, would Felicity really mind if she discovered her marriage wasn't legal? They haven't any children, have they?"

"Not that I've heard of. Conchita hasn't either."

"Then would they really mind, Mario and Felicity? They had this successful act. They were becoming famous and getting rich. I simply don't believe Mario would break it. I don't believe he would drown his whole fortune and future, quite apart from what he felt for Felicity. I know I wouldn't."

"Calculating bitch, aren't you, love?" Tim said, raising the hand he held to kiss the palm and then each finger separately.

"He'd be more likely to drown Conchita," Sally said, conclusively.

After a pause for thought Tim said, "I don't believe Conchita bribed the bar steward, though I hear he's rather a buddy of hers. Someone wants to stop my inquisitive prowlings. As I've done nothing in that line on the ship, except listen to Mrs Fairbrother and the other biddies nattering, it must be my activities on shore. Which brings me to two, possibly three possibilities."

"You've never told me a single thing about what you did in Bridgetown or why you didn't come back on board there or why you turned up again in Trinidad. I don't really know anything about you, do I?"

"Don't start now," he said. "We've all the time in the world for flash-backs. But not now. Just now I want to know who put the oleander in my drink."

"Was that what it was?"

"Yes. If you're any the wiser, which I'm not. Doc says an irritant poison like arsenic. Possibly yellow oleander."

"You were certainly yellow when I found you. Greenish yellow."

He made a face of extreme disgust.

"Callous harpy! To remind me! My God, why did

He give you that face and figure?"

She was happy enough to be unrepentant.

"I thought you thought Sir John had switched drinks," she said, pursuing the argument.

"He did. We were next to each other and we each had a gin and tonic. But he ordered first. I remembered that later."

"I see. You mean when he ordered he didn't know you were going to have the same tipple? So if he put poison in his drink he couldn't palm it off on you without your noticing. Or not for sure."

"Exactly."

"Then someone else wanted to poison Sir John."

"Presumably. I think the old boy isn't too strong. Certainly he's upset all ways just now. I think it would have finished him. It bloody well nearly finished me."

"Oh darling, don't! I can't bear to remember finding you. I know I tried to be funny over it just now. It wasn't funny at all. I thought at first you were dead. Then dying. I've never been more terrified in my life."

"Wiry," Tim said, stroking the head that had now sunk against his shoulder. "That's what my Auntie Flo always said when I was attacked by 'flu or measles or something. 'Nothing'll put him down,' she said, 'He's wiry.'"

"Oh Tim," Sally said. "You're as kinky as they come, but I really do love you."

Feeling he could not just yet do justice to his own feelings Tim shut his eyes. When Sally gently lifted her head she found that his hand had slipped from hers. He was asleep.

The unexpected call at Kingston, the main purpose of which was to renew the ship's supply of certain medical antidotes and also convey material to the excellent labs of the University Hospital, provided an opportunity for the medical travellers to disembark a few days earlier than they expected. Ian and Helen, however, decided that as they had paid to go to the Bahamas and fly back to Jamaica from there, it would be a pity to miss a piece of sight-seeing they were unlikely ever to repeat. So they stayed on board when their colleagues left, rather to Dr McRae's relief, for he believed Tim's attacker was still with them and might attempt to strike again.

Captain Crowthorne thought the same. He had manned the head of the gangway himself that morning to watch those who went ashore. At his side the Purser was making notes of them. If any did not return, apart from the medicos, he intended to tell the local police. But he was disappointed. His flock, with the advertised exceptions, returned, so he sailed again for the Bahamas with his anxiety unrelieved.

Though it was unrelieved it was, in a large measure, clarified during the next twenty-four hours. Sally and Tim had not been slow to reach the same conclusion as Captain Crowthorne. The would-be killer, perhaps already a murderer, was still on board. There were several passengers who might fear Tim on account of his profession.

"I don't know what you mean," Sally told him.

They were playing a very gentle game of quoits on the foredeck, only speaking at intervals when they happened to be standing close together. At this remark Tim abandoned the game and walked to the rail where Sally joined him.

"Too tiring?" she asked tenderly.

"You can say that again," he answered, loud enough to satisfy the Newbuckles who were approaching.

"Tim's too tired to finish," Sally said to them. "Do take over."

She and Tim moved further off to lean again on the rail watching the flying fish glitter from wave to wave.

"My profession," Tim said, picking up the threads of his argument where Sally showed her need of explanation. "A chap with a guilty conscience might think, knowing I was a journalist, that I had seen a photo of him or read an account or seen a tele interview of him some-

117

where. Provided he had ever had newspaper publicity."

"Well, have you?" Sally asked and added, "You might have explained that before."

"If there's one thing I'll never let you into," Tim said, "it's the dirtier kind of news story."

"You haven't answered my question."

"There isn't an answer. At least, not a real one. But there are several characters on this ship, among the passengers, who saw me wandering around on shore, both at Bridgetown and Port of Spain. Not to mention Conchita, of course. But I'm inclined to count her out of this."

"Good," said Sally, who had by now begun to feel rather sorry for the stewardess. "So what are you going to do about it?"

"I've not quite decided."

"You could tell me who they are, these sinister bods. Then I could keep an eye on them, too."

"I've told you," Tim said, pushing himself away from the rail. "You're out of this as far as I'm concerned."

Sally felt anger rising but told herself that convalescents were always difficult, contrary, depressed, maddening to look after. And must be indulged.

"You needn't bottle up that temper of yours," Tim said smiling. "Just because I'm convalescent. I know what I'm doing, it may be a bit risky and I'm not going to have it touching you. So I think I'll go and lie down for a bit. No, stay where you are. Tell them you sent me in. Yes, my darling, you tell them that."

He waved to the Newbuckles and walked away to the iron staircase, moving slowly, carefully, as if measuring out his strength to last the distance to his cabin. Sally, remembering his quick alert movements before the poisoning, felt a sharper pang of grief and pity and anxiety than she had ever felt in her short life. The Newbuckles saw her distress as they finished their game and went up to her.

"He's a lot better, isn't he?" Mrs Newbuckle said.

"But we thought you were very sensible to send him in. He's lost a lot of weight, hasn't he? What was it? A virus?"

"I expect so," Sally answered. "Dr McRae hasn't told me exactly." She blushed at this lie and the Newbuckles glanced at each other deciding upon quite another cause for the girl's embarrassment.

Mrs Newbuckle patted Sally's arm.

"We can guess how you feel," she said.

Sally groaned inwardly. So that was what they all would imagine as soon as Mrs Newbuckle had had time to spread her views of the little scene she and Fred Newbuckle had witnessed that morning. God defend her from ever getting mixed up in a small, restricted community again. No outer suburb for her and Tim. No gossiping neighbours in a Close, a Precinct, an Avenue, an Estate. No . . .

She pulled herself up, conscious that she was still standing with the Newbuckles, silent, idiotically smiling, her cheeks still hot. She gave a stupid half laugh, made a feeble attempt at an excuse and almost ran away from them.

"A proper case," Mr Newbuckle chuckled indulgently.

Sally ate her lunch primly, speaking little. Tim was still having his meals taken to him in his cabin direct from the ship's kitchens and supervised by the head chef himself. After lunch Sally went back to her cabin and spent the usual siesta hours lying on her back and imagining various ways of presenting Tim to her relations. Aunt Hilda and Uncle Oswald in Bermuda would be easy. They were kind, tolerant, cosmopolitan. But the parents might be a bit sticky. A freelance journalist in his early thirties who had no very definite means of support. Still, there was the drama of this voyage he could write up when he had broken down the mystery. Because there was a continuing mystery. Every time it looked like turning into a simple story something like the poisoning attempt came to mix it up again. So Tim still had a big chance to establish himself, if only things happened the way he wanted.

While Sally lay on her bunk half asleep, dreaming of the future, Tim stood outside the door of Sir John Meadows's cabin on A deck waiting to hear if his request for an interview would be granted.

Lady Meadows had appeared first in answer to his knock. Neither she nor her husband were taking a real siesta she said, merely resting and reading. She did not ask him in but shut the door on him while she retreated. It was several minutes before she reopened it, this time with a book in her hand.

"Go in," she said, standing aside. "This is Mr Rogers, John. But of course we met him at dinner the first night out from Bermuda, didn't we?" She turned apologetically to Tim, then back to her husband. 'I'll be in the library if you want me," she said and went away.

"Sit down," Sir John said heavily. "You haven't been well, I hear. Gastric 'flu, wasn't it?"

"No, sir," Tim said. "I was poisoned—deliberately."

Sir John stared at him.

"Dear me," he said. He did not seem to be surprised or alarmed. Certainly not guilty.

"When I realised what had happened to me," Tim went on, "I remembered that you had switched our drinks at the bar that evening before dinner. Gin and tonic—both."

Sir John sat upright at once.

"You're not suggesting—"

"No," Tim said. "I'm not, though I admit I did at first."

"How dare—"

"I'll tell you if you'll let me."

The older man subsided. He waved a hand for Tim to continue.

"I remembered later that you had ordered your gin and tonic *before* I did mine. So you didn't get a duplicate in order to put something in it and palm it off on me."

"What a thing to imagine!"

"I've been in South America for nearly three years. Very strange things can happen there and in these islands."

"Well, go on."

"I think from the timing and other factors the poison must have been in your gin, or in the tonic poured into the gin. It could have been supplied by the bar steward, knowing or unknowing or by someone else at the bar slipping a prepared gin or a prepared tonic in place of the ship's supply."

Sir John nodded.

"There was the usual small knot of doubtful characters on my other side," he said. "You know who I mean?"

"I think I do. They play cards interminably and have tried to skin the young and unwary. I was warned by that rather splendid chap who's gone to risk his life among Papa Doc's thugs."

"Young Ford. Yes. He got stung, I believe."

"Thought he ought to be with it. Found it meant being with a good deal more than he bargained for—not only gambling but false pretences and downright theft."

"I'm afraid I told them what I thought of them."

Sir John stopped abruptly.

"And so—" Tim prompted.

"Not to the press, young man. I may have been hasty with these con men, but I'm very very cautious with your profession."

"I think you've told me what I want to know," Tim said gently. "I'm not trying to pry into your personal affairs. But those characters have a grudge against you and against me, I think. Perhaps they wanted to remove you and fixed your drink and I got it, the drink I mean, because you switched with mine by mistake. Perhaps they bent the bar steward and tried to do me deliberately. Seeing the sort of people they are, perhaps they got rid of Felicity Fennister because she knew too much about them."

"Yes," Sir John said. After a few minutes he got up. The interview was over. Tim could only rise in his turn and follow to the door.

"I'm glad you called," Sir John said. "Good of you to put it all straight to me. I admire that."

He held out his hand to shake Tim's. The young man was inclined to laugh at the formality but at the same time was touched by it.

"We'll both have to look out from now on," he said a little awkwardly.

Sir John smiled. His eyes were very bright.

"Oh well," he said. "Thanks to you I know now what to do. In time, too. We're due in at the Bahamas tomorrow, I believe."

Later that day when she and her husband were changing for dinner Lady Meadows said, "What did that young man want from you?"

"Simply to confirm a theory."

"I don't understand."

"I'm sorry. I'll put it all into simple language tomorrow after we've called at Nassau."

"I thought we were to stay there two days."

"The plan has been altered because we had to put in at Kingston."

Lady Meadows gave up. Her husband's long career in the Civil Service had built into him a reinforced concrete wall of discretion, unbreakable, insurmountable. She gave up. That sharp-eyed and lynx-eared old Mrs Fairbrother would probably tell her over a sherry in the lounge. She hurried on with her dressing and left her husband still struggling to tie his tie with sticky sweating fingers.

Mrs Fairbrother needed no prompting.

"I saw Sir John having an earnest tête-à-tête with Captain Crowthorne," she said. "I hope nothing is wrong."

"Wrong!" Lady Meadows was astonished. "What would be wrong?"

Mrs Fairbrother was not at all put out.

"Our young newshound seems to have recovered completely from his illness," she said. "He told me at tea that he had been talking to Sir John. I wondered if he had annoyed him."

"Enough to make John complain to the Captain?" Lady Meadows, who had wondered just that herself, tried to look severe. "Oh no, I shouldn't think so. We quite like these two young things. Sally is rather sweet."

"She seems to have fallen for Tim in a very big way," Mrs Fairbrother said complacently, pleased with her command of fairly recent slang.

This conversation did nothing to enlighten Lady Meadows. In fact she had to wait several days for full understanding.

But Sir John made a point of speaking to Mr Bernstein after dinner, when there was dancing again in the lounge. All the younger passengers were fully occupied. The bridge players had settled down at their usual table in the lounge bar. Mrs Fairbrother was talking to the Newbuckles and a married couple of Jamaicans who had joined the ship at Kingston.

"The library perhaps," Mr Bernstein said. "A little game there in quiet."

"Yes," Lady Meadows said. "We'll lead the way, Mrs Bernstein."

Sir John hung back, keeping Max Bernstein beside him.

"A breath of air first," he suggested, making off in the opposite direction to the women. "We can go round the outside and meet them at the library door."

Mr Bernstein glanced behind him at the bridge players.

"Yes," he said. As he had told Lottie, the time would come.

But not quite as he expected.

"I wanted a word with you in private," Sir John said when they were alone, feeling a cool air blowing from the port beam. "About those swine in there."

123

"Meaning our bridge experts, swindlers—"

"Blackmailers," said Sir John.

"So." Mr Bernstein looked out to sea.

"They are known among the Islands," Sir John went on. "I took the trouble to confirm it in Bridgetown. I think they suspected this, but they were more disturbed by young Rogers. He rumbled them too."

"So," Mr Bernstein repeated, turning now to look at Sir John.

"I intended to string them along till I could get them picked up at Bermuda, but they went for Rogers in a big way. Nearly succeeded, too, from what Crowthorne tells me."

"So now you have acted, or Captain Crowthorne will act. Why do you tell me this?"

"Because I want you to know their grounds for attempted blackmail."

"It is not at all necessary. Please."

"I think it is. My son was arrested in England for having and selling drugs. He got a suspended sentence and a heavy fine. He is in hospital to cure his addiction. We came on this cruise to avoid the sympathy of our friends. My wife— Well, I couldn't face having it spread round the ship. There's been too much talk already about my going ashore without her, but those brutes want cash and with the allowance and that . . ."

They had moved slowly forward while Sir John was speaking and were now near the door that led in beside the library.

"You will not be offended, I hope," Max Bernstein said, "if I suggest you and Lady Meadows go ashore with me next time as my guests."

"Thanks very much," Sir John said. "Extremely kind."

"I am a banker's son," Mr Bernstein said. "Please also consider me your banker—for, shall we say—the overdraft—until you are in touch again with your own funds. I have—interests in Nassau."

"My dear fellow," said Sir John. "I really only wanted

you to know what the blackmail was about. In case—"

"I understand."

"Don't think I'm not grateful." Sir John's voice had become very low and gruff. "You've relieved my mind no end."

When they were going to bed that night Mrs Bernstein said, "So you were right, Max. Sir John was wanting to borrow money."

"Not exactly," Max answered. "He wanted to tell me why he has none left at present. The foreign exchange laws are very difficult and very complicated. So beautiful on paper and so silly in practice."

"You will lend him money, then?"

Mr Bernstein spoke very gently.

"We must never forget, my Lottie, that it is not possible for us to repay in our lifetime all we have been given by these English."

CHAPTER XII

All those passengers who had not been aware of the strange events taking place on *Selena*, who had not heard the gossip or had disregarded it, who had kept to their own groups or had avoided all but their own partners, were very disappointed when the ship anchored off Nassau to find that they could not immediately go ashore. What was the point, they grumbled, assembling on B deck as usual with shopping lists, dark glasses in place, beach clothes and even beach umbrellas, to find the town and those delicious beaches as far off as they were before breakfast.

The ship's officers, very inadequately briefed, did their best to reassure them. But the excuses were feeble; the customers were not satisfied.

"What's up, do you know?" Sally asked Tim.

"I can guess," he answered.

They were right at the back of the queue, which was in many ways an advantage, for they could stand up against the rail and command a good view, by leaning over, of the whole of the landward side of the ship.

"Will passengers please return to their cabins or to the lounge," the Chief Officer shouted through a megaphone. "You will be told when we have been allocated a berth and may go in. At present we have to wait. These are orders from the Port Authorities. Ladies and gentlemen —please!"

A few of those appealed to, mostly passengers who could see nothing for the press of bodies ahead, did turn and push their way from the crowd. But most stayed behind and thereby caused some confusion greatly to their disadvantage.

"Look shorewards," Tim said, not pointing and speaking in a low voice. "That launch just putting out towards us. Do you see what I see?"

"Immigration and customs as usual, I suppose," Sally answered. "But why the—did you see that glint?— Rifles with bayonets fixed? Just like the film of a badly managed *coup d'état*!"

"Which is just what I expect to happen. I think—" he looked behind him where the queue was at its thinnest. "I think upstairs before the bullets fly. Come on."

They shot back along B deck, climbing to the one above which seemed to be totally empty and rushed along until they came to the spot directly above the collected crowd. The launch was coming alongside. It disappeared from view. There were shouts, orders, then silence.

"Oh hell!" Tim cried. "They've taken them in where we can't see, for'ard or aft. Unless—"

He made off forward, Sally following. He passed the limit marked for passengers, he climbed the remaining steps to the topmost deck of all, above the bridge.

"We still can't see them," Sally complained.

"We can hear though. Listen!"

There were cries now, chiefly rising from the place they had left on B deck, where the bulk of the passengers had disregarded the Chief Officer's plea. The shouts rose in volume; there were screams too, from frightened women.

"I'm glad we came up here," Sally said weakly. "Were they soldiers or police? Have they come for poor Conchita?"

"I hope not," Tim said. Then he pointed. "There! Watch that speed boat! The one with the water skier! He's gone over. They're picking him up. I wonder!"

He began to scramble aft, keeping bent double, dodging behind life-boats. Sally followed, for the speed boat had started off again at full throttle, its bows lifting, the spray and the wake a white obscuring cloud.

"Now!" Tim said. "Now watch our stern sheets. There! I thought so. Two of the bastards!"

Two figures in bathing trunks were moving along the lower deck towards the rail. They paid no attention to three members of *Selena's* crew, who in turn paid no attention to them. They were used to the queer ways of passengers.

But just as the bathers reached the rail loud voices called to them to stop. The crew turned and stared. Tim, suddenly in action, began winding his ciné-camera. One of the men sprang to the rail, leaping up on it, dived and disappeared. The other, slower, was brought down by a single shot and crumpled to the deck as the police officers dashed forward.

"Oh!" Sally moaned. "Horrible! Horrible!"

"He's made it!" Tim shouted. "That speed boat's picked him up. There it goes! They'll never get it!"

He was right. More shots were fired, but all into the sea. The speed boat, mingling with other craft, was soon indistinguishable. It would be difficult to pick out one special water-skier from so many who were swinging in their graceful curves on the calm waters outside the harbour.

"I hope he isn't dead." Sally, still white-faced, still shaky, put an arm through Tim's.

"I couldn't care less," he answered. "He had it coming to him. They all did. Captain Crowthorne must have laid this on. He and Sir John between them, I wouldn't wonder."

"Sir John? Sir John Meadows? What's he got to do with it?"

"I wouldn't know. You'd better ask Mrs Fairbrother."

Sally burst into tears. It was bad enough to have a recent death involving her cabin, a recent attempted murder of the man she knew she loved, without having to see a brutal killing, or near killing, however criminal the victim.

Tim comforted her, gaining much pleasure in the process. He was sufficiently old-fashioned to welcome signs of feminine weakness in the girl he had just decided to marry. It was not until later that he became surprised at this sudden decision and told himself it needed further thought before he passed it on to Sally.

When she was able to lift her head and dry her eyes they both realised that their next move must be to find the men who had come on board and give an account of what they had seen. Tim had noticed while Sally's face was hidden against his shoulder that a tarpaulin had been thrown over the crumpled figure below the rail. So he led her away out of sight of it as soon as he could and having taken her to her cabin and left her there, went in search of a ship's officer, any officer who could put him in touch with the men he sought.

Before long he was taken to the office behind the Purser's desk, where he found Captain Crowthorne, the Purser himself and two of the officials who had come out to the ship.

"We've been looking for you everywhere," the Captain said, with a relieved smile. "You were not among the passengers when we managed to herd them into the lounge. Nor Miss Combes."

"Miss Combes was with me," Tim said. "We were on the top deck and—"

"The devil you were!" said Captain Crowthorne, growing very red beneath his tan.

"Sorry, sir, if that was out of order," Tim answered coolly. "Actually I was afraid of a rough-house when I saw the search party's launch, so we pulled out."

"Tell us what you saw from your vantage point," suggested the leader of the officials, a grey-haired man with a military bearing and a quiet English voice.

Tim described it all, the escape attempt, the successful dive, the failure of the slower man, his killing by shooting.

"The other got away?"

'He's a first class swimmer. And his buddies in the speed boat certainly know their job. Not easy to come in that close on the weather side and pick them up and get out of range in time. Your chaps were not so hot firing down at the head in the water as they were firing across the deck. Lucky they didn't knock off any of *Selena*'s crew while they were about it. Incidentally I've got a ciné record of the whole thing."

There was a minute's silence of sheer disapproval. But Captain Crowthorne's colour had returned to its normal mid-brown and there was a distinct light of amusement in the eyes he turned on Tim.

"We have therefore accounted for three of those four men," the senior Nassau officer said. "One we arrested in his cabin. His friend, who shared that cabin got away and must have warned the other pair. One of those is dead and the other. . . ." He stopped, shrugging slightly.

"You will pick up when he tries to land from the boat."

"That is what we hope."

"Which leaves one still unaccounted for?" Tim asked.

"Correct."

"And still on board, presumably?"

Captain Crowthorne answered that one.

"I think you are entitled to know. You gave Sir John the confidence to come to me with his story. We have discussed this fourth man. Search parties of my officers and crew visited all the passenger cabins and corridors, lounges and so forth before we let the passengers leave the main lounge. They didn't object. The sound of firing shook them considerably."

"I bet it did," Tim could not help interrupting.

"However, we drew a blank. So what we propose is this. We shall go into a harbour berth while I still have the passengers cooped up. With our friends here we shall watch the ship and the wharf. If there is no attempt to escape, no suspicious character seen on board or on shore we shall conclude that he has already slipped through and we shall sail in the morning early."

"And the passengers?" Tim asked.

"Are at the moment looking at a film," answered Captain Crowthorne.

"Including Miss Combes? I left her at her cabin door."

130

"I asked my cadet officer, Mr Groves, to take her up to the lounge to see it. And to see that she stayed there."

Tim's face paled with anger which gave the Captain a certain satisfaction. He hoped for an explosion that might give him some excuse to retaliate for the young man's insolent invasion of those parts of the ship forbidden to passengers unless invited. But all Tim said was, "If we're going ashore I take it I shall have time to phone my paper with the day's news?"

"You will do no such thing!" Captain Crowthorne shouted as his patience left him.

"These gentlemen will be leaving, I take it?" Tim asked, turning to look at the grey-haired man.

The latter smiled.

"Indeed we will. In our launch immediately. To make the further arrangements that will be necessary and relieve Captain Crowthorne of the corpse of a much sought-after criminal."

"I rather thought as much," Tim said and suggested a name.

"It is clear you know far too much to be allowed to call your editor," the grey-haired man said, smiling. "Until we have this fourth man we want no publicity."

"You won't take me ashore in your launch?"

"Nothing would suit me better," Captain Crowthorne said, "provided you keep him in Nassau until after I've sailed."

"If I did go ashore you wouldn't let me come back?" Tim asked.

"I'm damned if I would."

"I've paid my fare to Bermuda."

"My owners have cleared me for any action I take."

It was stalemate and Tim knew it. The faces round him had all grown stony. His help was forgotten. Only it hadn't been his direct help. He had merely triggered off old John Meadows. The old boy would get any public reward that was going. More likely the whole thing would be hushed up. Sir John's blackmail must have been for something serious, after all.

"If I'm not allowed to contact my paper and earn my living, I might as well watch your blasted film,"he said, getting to his feet.

"Of course," Captain Crowthorne told him. "If the gentlemen don't need you at present as a witness."

A murmured chorus agreed with the Captain. Tim left the office nearly knocking over the second wireless officer who was waiting outside. He stepped back when he saw Tim.

"Are you waiting to take me up to the lounge?" Tim asked bitterly.

"No. Actually I'm to hand in a message we've just had."

"You wouldn't like to put me in touch with my editor? New York would do?" Tim asked eagerly. "This story . . ."

The wire officer nodded. Worth considering, surely.

"Half a jiffy while I take this in," he said.

He was more than half a jiffy. Captain Crowthorne had asked him if he'd met Tim outside the door and on hearing that he had, ordered him to take that young man to the lounge, see he went in and did not come out immediately. And to take no urgent message from him in code or otherwise.

"No go," the wireless officer told Tim. "Sorry, old boy. He asked about you and gave orders. No flies on our old man. Thinks of everything."

"Don't tell me that's why he is where he is," Tim groaned. "I know it all. I'll find my way to the films. Don't bother."

"Orders," murmured the wireless officer, following Tim to the stairs.

By nightfall *Selena* was on her way again, her problem unresolved. Unless the fourth man of the fraud gang had got away right at the start while the passengers were still seething about the decks, he was still on board, a hunted man and dangerous.

How dangerous Tim learned a few hours later when

Conchita came knocking at his cabin door. As he opened it she came quickly in, shutting it behind her.

"He is here, that man," she told him. "He will kill you!"

Tim, already in pyjamas on his way to bed felt more anger than fear at this announcement. He had no doubt that it was true. Conchita, thanks to Sally's kindness to her, was no longer gunning for either of them. Disillusionment, at least as far as he himself was concerned, would come later.

"Where is he?"

She shrugged.

"Now—at this moment—who can tell? He has been seen. That is all. There is one who helped him. They make their arrangements long time."

"Probably."

He stood thinking. The man must be made to expose himself, then be taken. No doubt he would be watching and the whole body of officers would be watching too, waiting for him to appear. But perhaps not the deck hands or the engine room—seeing he had a friend—or was it more than one?

"How do you know this?" he asked. "Why should I believe you?"

She spread her hands.

"You please yourself," she said. "I tell you for Miss Combes. Danger for her too."

Well, if this was a trap, better to spring it, Tim thought and quickly. He held out his hand.

"Give me your master keys," he said. "I will go to Miss Combes."

Conchita took them from her pocket, handed them over, struck her hands together as if she wiped them clean of any further responsibility. She turned on her heel and moved out of the cabin as quietly and swiftly as she had come in.

When she had gone Tim rapidly exchanged his pyjama trousers for a pair of slacks, slipped into their pockets the keys and a small weapon he had found useful from time to time in his South American wanderings, and leaving the light on in his cabin, went silently along the empty corridor outside and up to B deck.

He met no one on the way, saw no one. The fanlights of most of the cabins were dark, their inmates presumably sleeping. But his solitary passage was no guarantee that he had not been seen. He had passed several open service doors and cubby holes, also in darkness, from which hidden eyes could have watched him. But he reached his objective unchallenged, used Conchita's key and moved swiftly into Sally's cabin.

He said as soon as he was inside, "Don't put the light on. It's me, Tim."

He had taken it for granted she would be awake. He was right. He said quickly. "No time to explain but I think we're going to have a visit. Here. Take some clothes into the shower and put them on. Stay there."

His eyes were now adjusting to the darkness, which was not absolute, since the light from the corridor, though subdued, showed through the narrow glass above the door. He saw Sally slip out of her bunk and gather an armful of clothes off a chair beside it. She had not spoken a word.

His heart rose in admiration and tenderness at this easy agreement, this swift understanding and trust. As she passed him he caught her close for a second.

"Bless you, my darling," he whispered, cutting short the kiss he would have given much to prolong into a more satisfying exchange.

But this brief embrace gave him an idea. After Sally had shut her bathroom door he snatched her top pillow and added it to those on the other bunk under the window. A few more lumpings together of sheets and bolsters and he had managed the effect he wanted.

He had just enough time to join Sally in the darkness of the bathroom when a thin shaft of light crept over the carpet in the cabin. Someone incredibly quiet, immensely skilled, was opening the door. Sally's keys were in the room, Conchita's in his own pocket. Was another bent steward in the racket or was this a practised thief? Holding Sally with his left hand to reassure her, Tim slipped his other fingers round the silent weapon in his right hand pocket.

CHAPTER XIV

The fight that followed was disappointing. Or so Tim insisted afterwards.

To begin with the enemy failed to shut the cabin door behind him. Instead he crept straight across to the bunk under the window and plunged the knife he held into the upper part of the bolster Tim had arranged there. Shocked by the ease with which the weapon sank into its target the would-be assassin jerked his arm back and across, to find himself showered with a heavy flight of feathers and torn fabric. In his astonishment he opened his mouth and drew a deep breath that carried with it such a parcel of down as made him choke and cough quite helplessly. In a moment Tim leaped on him from behind, wrenched the knife from his hand and bearing him to the ground sat on his legs and leaned on his arms while Sally turned on the cabin lights and ran to the half-open door to call for help.

"Don't shout!" Tim ordered. "Get something to tie the bastard's legs."

She had nothing suitable except a couple of scarves, large, silken and stretchy. Tim grumbled at their elastic nature, but he managed to secure his prisoner, who made surprisingly little fuss since he was still coughing feathers from his lungs. Indeed he watched with a faint air of derision. However, when he rolled over and tried to sit up, Tim pushed him down again. He had taken the precaution of fastening the man's hands behind his back. He now borrowed a third scarf to tie the ends of the other two together. The man twisted and fought as he did so, but was soon rendered properly helpless, still heaving, spitting with rage and bronchial disturbance, but only succeeding in tightening his bonds.

"What now?" Sally asked. "We can't keep him here. We don't want to, do we?"

The prisoner stopped cursing to listen. His voice was quite calm as he said, looking at Tim, "No, you do not want me to say how I came to this cabin. How I found the door open and imagined the room was empty and came in. How I found the lady was entertaining her lover. How he sprang up and attacked me for disturbing them — This you will not want me to explain. And so you will give me the money I need and let me go."

"The hell we will!" Tim laughed scornfully. "How do you account for your knife and the feathers you carved out of the pillow and then inhaled, poor sod. Not to mention the fact that you found us both up and fully dressed when you did realise your murderous attack had boobed. No blackmail this time, old son. Sally, I think you'd better see if you can find someone to clear away the rubbish."

He touched the prisoner gently with his foot to indicate that he included him in the disposable litter and the man strained at his bonds and began to chatter curses again in English and Spanish mixed.

Sally did not have to go far. No further than the corridor outside her door. Conchita was just arriving and behind her Dick Groves, looking anxious.

"I'm all right," said Sally, answering his look. "We've got the man. I mean the one that escaped and hid on board, not the one that the speed boat picked up."

Dick slipped past her without listening to the over-long explanation. He was accustomed to action first and explanations after. But he was as disappointed as Tim had been. The action was all over. The prisoner was securely, if humiliatingly, trussed up. Tim was standing over him, holding two knives.

"This one's his," Tim said. "No damage except to the bolster on the unoccupied bunk. He thought it was me — as he intended — or perhaps me and Sally."

She had come in again behind Dick and now laughed.

"He's just tried to blackmail us—because of Tim being here," she said.

Tim laughed and Dick smiled. A pretty feeble attempt he thought. Conchita had told him as they hurried along how she had warned Tim and helped him. Sally laughed again.

The man on the floor, desperate now, muttered "Yes, you filthy cow! The other one laughed, too!"

At that Conchita came close silently and struck him across the mouth.

Captain Crowthorne, who did not appear in the dining saloon at breakfast, made a short announcement on the intercom directly after the weather bulletin.

"Ladies and gentlemen," he said. "The slight difficulty at Nassau that cut short our recent stay there and prevented you all going ashore has been cleared up. Many of you will have noticed that we are heading back there now. We shall berth in an hour's time. We shall not leave again until tomorrow which will be our scheduled date for departure for Bermuda. Thank you."

A loud buzz of excited comment followed this announcement. There must have been very few passengers on board who had not grasped the real meaning of his words. Though nobody knew exactly what the four criminals were supposed to have done, far less who they really were, it was not too difficult, adding up what various people had really seen and subtracting from that the total of obvious fantasy, to conclude that two were out of the game, by arrest and death, before the police left the ship. One was known to have escaped in a speed boat. So that left one unaccounted for. Were they going back because Captain Crowthorne had heard he was arrested on shore? Or had he been found hiding on Selena and they were going back to deliver him up?

The passengers hurried through their breakfasts and went on deck. The land was near, they were proceeding quietly towards it. They approached, the usual manoeuvres followed, they berthed, the angled gangway was let down and fixed. Nothing had happened. It was all an anti-climax.

In fact it was Mrs Fairbrother who got the clearest picture of what actually happened, though not by any means the whole of it. She had avoided the restless crowds and taken refuge on A deck for a change, settling down at the after end above the swimming pool. There Sally found her.

"You don't look at all excited," Mrs Fairbrother said, "so I suppose you already know exactly what has happened to bring us back here so unexpectedly."

"Didn't you expect it?" Sally said. "I was sure you'd guess one of those thugs had escaped."

"Why yes. We all knew that."

"And hidden on board?"

"I wondered."

As Sally neither confirmed nor denied this, Mrs Fairbrother said, "Tell me, did you have a pillow fight in your cabin last night?"

Scarlet in the face Sally said, "Really! Who on earth would I be likely to— Anyway, why *pillow*? I don't think I've ever— It sounds like a school-girl story of pre-First World War."

"Which I read with pleasure," said Mrs Fairbrother. "My reason for asking is the quantity of feathers a steward was trying to suck up into a Hoover outside your cabin door. The door was open and I'm afraid I looked in and there were feathers *everywhere*. So pillow fight was the first thing that came into my head."

"Not *pillow*," said Sally. "But I oughtn't to say any more. Not at present. Tim would be furious if he knew I'd said as much."

"You needn't," Mrs Fairbrother told her. "Neither of you came to any harm, I trust."

"Oh no."

"Then I suppose—" Mrs Fairbrother looked away out to sea, considering. "I suppose, when I thought I heard

them taking a pilot on board very early this morning i
was really the other way round. Someone was taken int
the launch, *off* the ship."

"Did you know we'd turned round?"

"Oh, yes."

"Was there a launch?" Sally asked feebly. She had no
heard a thing early that morning. She had slept flat out a
soon as everyone had left her cabin and had woken wit
a jerk long after breakfast time. She had missed the
Captain's announcement and Tim had already left the
table. But the Chief Officer who was still there had
brought her up to date.

"I'm afraid I overslept again," Sally now explained t
Mrs Fairbrother. "I haven't seen Tim yet this morning
Perhaps—"

She broke off, afraid of saying too much, for the eage
look in Mrs Fairbrother's eyes had not diminished. In
deed her lively understanding had leaped a few more con
ventional barriers and to Sally's consternation she sai
brightly, "Now we shall have no more trouble, I hope
But I wonder who it was that hid that man. Do you
think possibly Conchita was at the bottom of it? Sh
hasn't been altogether cleared of the attempt on poor
Tim, has she? For interfering—journalistically, I mean
of course—with her personal affairs."

Sally had no answer to this and did not attempt t
give one. She sat quite silent until she could bear it n
longer, when she made a very lame excuse and wen
back to her cabin.

It was a question to which no one on board had as ye
an answer. Tim, who had spent an uncomfortable hour
with Captain Crowthorne immediately after Sally had
been left to herself, had no suggestions. He was able to
report Conchita's warning and her help in getting into
Sally's cabin quickly and quietly.

"Which puts paid to her employment on my ship," the
Captain said. 'Stewardesses who open doors for passengers
are out—definitely. Did you pay her?"

140

Tim stared.

"Pay? Why should I?"

Captain Crowthorne stared back.

"If Sally wanted me in her cabin she'd have given me her own key, wouldn't she?" Tim said. "You can cut that line. It isn't on. The warning was real. The crook arrived. You know what happened."

"Perhaps Conchita didn't expect you to win."

"I don't see how that would help him—attacking, even killing—a passenger."

"A journalist who already knew too much."

"As you will. But coming out into the open at all was crazy, wasn't it?"

"The man who was shot on deck was his brother," Captain Crowthorne said. "He *was* three parts crazy after dodging round the crew's quarters and the engine room for the best part of eight hours." The Captain sighed.

"I take it there's no objection to my going ashore this time?" Tim asked.

"Not my business. Our prisoner will be taken off before we go in. Customs and immigration will come aboard in the usual way. I expect you will be asked to make a statement to add to your former one."

"I must cable my story," Tim said doggedly.

"The story, as you call it, will have gone to the press hours before you can possibly get ashore."

"Not the whole story."

Captain Crowthorne had nothing more to say. As Tim left him he saw Conchita being led towards the office. They would get nothing from her, he thought. But would Crowthorne throw her out now? This was not what he himself wanted in the interests of his more important news, the mystery of Felicity Fennister's death. No, he did not want that black deed made clear until they were back in Bermuda. It occurred to him that though Captain Crowthorne was unlikely to get any useful information from Conchita, the Nassau police might have ways and means of producing some from the

141

venomous wriggling snake who had given such a lamentable performance on the floor of Sally's cabin.

He shuddered as he thought over the details of that scene. A knife is a knife, even in the most inefficient hands. Without Conchita— What might have happened did not bear thinking of. But the warning implied very dangerous knowledge. It disturbed him not a little to think how he had planned to reward Conchita before this night's events. A little only. The rich results for himself were worth the woman's discomfiture. He had already given up any thought of pinning murder upon either her or Mario Fenestri. The gang, for reasons not yet proved, must have been responsible for Felicity's disappearance. That was something else the Nassau police might extract from their prisoner. Their new prisoner. They had two now. To play one against the other, perhaps.

For the second time on this voyage Tim did not go to bed at all that night. After leaving the Captain he showered and dressed for going ashore. Then he sat down and wrote his account of the police raid on *Selena*, watched by him from the top deck. This included a detailed description of the water-skiing speed boat, the dramatic appearance and actions of the two crooks and the end of one of them.

Quite pleased with this effort Tim then wrote a separate account of the fight in Sally's cabin, being careful to keep the girl entirely out of it. As he finished this piece he was aware of the ship slowing down, of shouted orders, of voices far off and far below.

He was in time, leaning far over the rail on B deck, to see dimly the return of the police launch and to be aware of movement on it and aboard *Selena*. He was also aware, in the now lightening sky, of an outline above the horizon that was not cloud or mirage. He went back to his cabin to write a third piece on the final arrest of the fourth member of the bridge-playing ring.

He was allowed on shore without many questions asked

and with no restrictions. After all, his passport gave his profession and was quite in order. Also, as Captain Crowthorne had suggested and he himself had known from the beginning, the Press had already got the main lines of the story and he found, when he did get ashore among the first to leave the ship, had already dug out the news that the bridge gang was known in the Caribbean as a dangerous lot, plundering cruise ships, tipped off by members of crews in their pay, protected by the unwillingness of the ordinary tourists both to upset their holidays and also to display their foolishness in being conned. Also, in the more sinister cases, their submission without public protest to blackmail.

Tim did not mind these revelations. He had suspected them from the start, but had not had the means to confirm his suspicions. Now he had very much more juicy meat to offer. He got in touch with his editor in Bermuda: he gave the substance of his articles: he was told to get them off that day by airmail which would deliver them in Bermuda in a few hours, long before *Selena* would arrive there. Tim's suggestion of an advance for expenses was met with prompt agreement. In a very self-satisfied mood he returned to the ship at lunch time. He would pick up Sally and go to town in a very big way.

But Sally was not on board. His frantic search for her lasted until he found Mrs Fairbrother, who told him she had gone with Ian and Helen to see them off at the airport. But first to visit one of the beaches.

"It was the reason they stayed on board instead of taking the opportunity to land when we put in at Jamaica," Mrs Fairbrother reminded him.

"I know. They were booked to come on to the Bahamas."

"They had until tonight. Such a shame we stayed at sea most of the time."

Tim agreed, while feeling it might be quite good for Ian to discover that even the best-laid plans did not always succeed. He thanked Mrs Fairbrother and went disconsolately away wondering where he could begin to look for Sally. It seemed to him now that unless he could tell her about his success and share its profits, life was no longer worth living.

Abandoning all thought of lunch he went ashore again, found the inevitable seller of maps established at the inevitable taxi rank and having bought what he needed, hired a cab to begin his search. He sat beside his driver, a cheerful brown-faced, multiracial character and explained his urgent quest.

"This girl swim?" his driver asked.

"Yes. So do the friends she's with."

"They just swim? Not surf ride, not water-ski?"

It occurred to Tim suddenly that there might be some interest in water-skiing.

"Take me where there's water-skiing," he said.

So it came about that he arrived on the beach in his taxi in time to see the conclusion of the last episode in the story of the bridge gang.

Ian, who had done water-skiing for several summers from the English West Country resorts, had insisted upon performing off Nassau. He hired a speed boat with a local driver and tackle. Helen and Sally preferred to swim.

Towards the end of his hired time Ian insisted upon them coming out with him. So they were in the boat when Sally recognised the craft she had seen near *Selena* the day before. She also recognised the man balancing on his skis, riding them superbly well. She cried out excitedly.

"He's a pro," their American driver told them, swinging wide to give Ian a good turn before taking him in for his last straight run. "Been away this last week or two. Ran out to that cruise liner yesterday and there's waves out there. That guy can do anything."

"He's the man they want," Sally shouted. "The man that got away!"

144

"Now, sister," their driver said. "Quit bawling and sit or you'll have us over."

But Sally continued to shout and wave because she had seen a small launch dodging out from the shore. There were uniformed men in it, two standing up, one with binoculars, the other with a rifle.

Helen grabbed Sally and pulled her down to the floor-boards.

"Pick Ian up," she ordered. "And get us out of here!"

"Trouble—huh?" said the American laconically. He slowed his boat, turned round to signal to Ian who came on indignantly until the tow slackened and he had to sink into the water. Even then he paddled out sideways with the rope to keep it off the propeller as the boat did a tight turn.

The warning yell came too late. The skier, the American so much admired, had at last realised the significance of the approaching launch and perhaps also that it was guided by Sally. It was Ian who yelled as the hunted man bore down upon them, his black clad form and goggled face terrifying in its concentration. His speed boat creamed away to turn him, to let him skim past, inches from them, dealing death if he could from the pistol they saw he carried at his belt.

But neither he nor his driver had expected Ian's boat to stop. He had made his turn to pass them, not to find them directly in his path.

Ian dived, swimming away frantically under water. Helen and Sally flattened themselves in the bottom of the boat. The American spun the wheel and drove his boat to meet the charging skier head on.

But the man sprang, a perfectly timed leap, perfectly executed, clear of the stationary boat's bows, jerking round as he landed in answer to his own boat's lateral pull that had preserved his tow from fouling. It was breath-taking, it was magnificent. And ahead of him now was the police launch, turning across his path.

Tim was among those who watched the launch come in

to the skiers' jetty and unload a covered figure to an ambulance waiting beyond the sand. He stayed for the boat carrying his friends. The girls went off without speaking to find their clothes. Ian, who had paid in advance, thanked the American and turned away.

"They were out hunting for him," Ian said. "Must have had a tip-off. Sally recognised him. By his movements it must have been. That may have helped the dicks but they'd spotted him in the end. He was armed but that didn't help him."

"What happened?"

"The launch took him. Shame in a way. I've never seen such a performance. But he had to let go and dive and he wasn't clear. The propeller of the launch took his leg. Femoral artery, I imagine. Dead when they got him out. Worse than a shark."

"About the same," Tim said. "I saw it once. The blood—"

"Don't tell me. We saw it all. The girls— We'd better go to them."

What it is to be a budding surgeon, Tim thought irreverently, watching the confident brown back stride away. He followed slowly, feeling sick, his heart aching for Sally, who had taken a helping part in this second, this latest death.

CHAPTER XIV

He found her crying miserably, alone, waiting for him. As he put his arms round her to draw her close he asked indignantly, "Where are the others? Why have they gone off without you?"

"They wanted me to go with them," she sobbed. "They said you wouldn't come while there was a story to pick up. They said—"

She could not finish the sentence, but he knew, with a twinge of shame, that it was true. He *had* waited to see the end of the drama, to make quite sure he had the facts. He *had* given first place to his profession. But what the hell? If she married him she'd have to get used to that. It wouldn't put her in second place; only in a totally different one.

"You'll have to get used to that," he murmured aloud, still holding her, stroking her half dried hair.

"To what?" she asked, lifting her head to stare at him.

Disconcerted, he tried to explain without actually turning what he said into a definite proposal of marriage. Sally listened, amused enough by his flounderings to ease her mind and her feelings away from the dreadful scene she had been forced to witness, when the dying, mutilated wretch had been lifted from the water and the sea ran red between their boat and the police launch.

In the end she said, to end his stammerings, "You don't have to apologise for doing your job. Let me go, Tim. I think I'll go back to *Selena*."

"You certainly will not. If you're ready you'll come with me and we'll get off this beach and find somewhere to eat. I'm back on the staff of a newspaper, I'd have you know. Free-lancing is all very well in its way but for sober middle-aged life give me a secure job any time."

"My poor Tim," Sally cried. "You're talking like a Government Social Security pamphlet. Or are you practising the kind of thing your boss favours?"

"Oh my God," Tim groaned, "is it as bad as that already?"

Away from the beach they found Ian and Helen still unfed, still searching, so Tim took charge of the party, having been to Nassau before, and the four had an excellent lunch together, criminal horrors forgotten for the time being.

"I suppose they deserved all they got," Ian said to Tim, as they walked together towards the ship, the girls moving more slowly some way behind.

"The two that have died are the lucky ones," Tim said, "but perhaps the police are not allowed to be quite so crude here as they are in some places I've been."

"What's Jamaica like in that respect?" Ian asked. "Now they've got independence. It may affect me at the hospital."

"They flog the petty villain," Tim told him. "But by and large they're modelled on the British justice they had before. The University and Hospital are fine. Good houses for hospital staff, too. You ought to enjoy it."

"I hope so," Ian said a little doubtfully. Helen had been hysterical in the boat going ashore after the accident. She had blamed him for not going to the rescue of the unfortunate skier. But how could he? Their American boatman had refused outright to go anywhere near the launch. Anyway, he'd seen them try to fix a tourniquet, but with only a stump of thigh, the femoral artery cut through, any treatment not absolutely immediate would have been useless. The poor wretch was below water too, for nearly four minutes off and on as they dragged him clear; screaming at first when he came up, probably inhaling water when he went down again.

Apart from being useless any interference he might

148

have insisted on would have wrecked their schedule hopelessly. They might have been kept in Nassau as witnesses. As it was he and Helen had got away in time. If Sally didn't mind being a witness the police still had her to question. And the American owner of the speed boat he'd hired. Of course he'd be the one called upon. He knew the whole gang—or so he'd implied. Might be showing off, of course. Tim listened to all this, impassive, making no comment.

Ian collected his luggage as soon as he got back to the ship. He and Helen then left quietly for the airport. Tim and Sally watched them from the rail of B deck.

"I didn't think much of him today," Sally said. "All that energy and bossiness went out like a wet match. One little fizz and—nothing."

"I expect he needs his equipment round him," Tim said, quite seriously. "I've seen these specialists before. Not surgeons, actually. But the highly skilled in a trade. You need imagination in an emergency—"

He broke off, staring into the distance, his mouth open.

"What is it?" Sally exclaimed. "What have you seen? Where?"

"Only in my head," Tim answered. "Not to worry— Christ, it's hot! I'd like to swim. Here on board," he added, seeing Sally's grimace of horror.

"You can't. They're cleaning the pool."

"Hell! It had better be a shower then."

"I'm going to find Mrs Fairbrother," Sally said. "She'll expect it and she's so very soothing."

"You do that," Tim told her. "See you in the bar when it's open."

Sally nodded. "I'll watch your glass and see no one switches it," she said and walked away.

His glass was safe now, Tim thought, the bridge four was eliminated. The blackmailers gone. But perhaps not the whole gang. There was still the question of Conchita's tip-off to him and so presumably at least one doubtful and indiscreet member of the crew. Had this

149

side of the affair been sorted out and cleared up? How could he discover the truth of it? Not by direct questioning. Not by going to Captain Crowthorne again. Sir John? Not very hopeful. The police? Definitely not, unless they came after him for today's development.

Following the programme he had proposed for himself Tim went to his cabin, stripped off and got under the shower. When he had dressed again he sat down with pencil and paper to write out the significance of the various facts he had collected since his assignment began. 'Find out what really happened to Mrs Fennister,' the editor had said. He had not yet done so.

But as he sat, not writing anything, simply going over in his mind all that had happened on the ship and on shore since he left Bermuda, he found two memories recurring, two insistent trifles beating against his strong common-sense resistance to what they implied. One was the fantastic thought that had come to him while he stood with Sally on the deck half an hour before. The other was the reaction of the man he had defeated in Sally's cabin when he had tried to insult her and she had laughed. The man had said, "The other one laughed too." He had spoken in a way that suggested both amazement and disgust at Sally's attitude. She had not given a damn for the crook's feeble last-minute attempt at blackmail because she couldn't care less what the world thought about her relationship with himself. The other passengers, the western world of today, simply did not care how the young behaved together, apart from the production of illegitimate children. And that more for the material complications involved than the moral position and the cruel wrong done to a new innocent helpless individual. No. Sally thought it just funny to be threatened with utterly futile exposure, especially as the wretch had misread the situation. She had laughed.

"The other one laughed too." Was that Felicity? Were the muttered words another threat? You can laugh, so did she and look what happened to her? If she had laughed at attempted blackmail it was because the crooks thought Mario was not legally her husband, and she didn't give a damn. She laughed as Sally had laughed. As he had felt like laughing himself if he had had enough breath left after the fight to do so.

Had Mario laughed? Very likely. He was keeping Conchita quiet until they reached Bermuda. Perhaps, in spite of the laughter he was stringing the crooks along too. And at Bermuda? Tim had seen him for less than five minutes. He had been polite, cold, distant, unhelpful, in the single interview he had given to the Press. There had been no mention whatever of Conchita.

But it must have been Conchita who had given her past to the gang. Did the news of Mario's earlier marriage, of his later bigamy, come to Felicity from them or from Conchita or from Mario himself? 'She laughed.' The suicide note in Felicity's own handwriting, vouched for by her sister, Mrs Longford, hardly matched that gay indifference. So what did it signify? If it was false, how was it false? Who had lied? Who was still lying?

At the end of an hour Tim had written nothing, concluded nothing. But he was more than ever obsessed by his problem, more than ever inclined to break away from common-sense into the uncertain realm of fantasy. He left the paper and pencil on the table and went up on deck.

There was hardly anyone about. He thought that he had been wrestling with his problems for hours but his watch told him it was no more than three o'clock. A blistering afternoon sun pouring down upon the open deck drove him upwards in search of shade and air. He found himself on A deck at the point where passengers were stopped by a notice from invading the bridge. The notice he had ignored the day before, taking Sally with him above to the top deck.

He paused today at the notice, turning to the rail and looking down. As he moved closer to lean over his foot struck an object below the rail, which turned out to be, when he had turned it over, a piece of wood, a Wet Paint notice.

He then remembered having seen it standing against the rail with the message clearly visible on his very first visit to that part of the ship after he had hurried on board just in time. He remembered thinking, 'Why the hell all this punctuality if they'd time to start titivating?'

He had forgotten this small episode entirely; now the odd little fact came back to him, so he began to inspect the rail very closely, to discover where the paint had been needed.

It was a small area about twelve inches wide. The strip of the top rail, the structures below it, and the wire netting covering the gaps. The fresh paint below the rail had been applied only to the outside, seaward-facing parts. Something had scraped the top rail and scratched a wider area below it. What? More important, why? Apart altogether from general rules of smartness, particularly on A deck where the wealthy passengers travelled.

Where the Fennisters had their cabin. No, that was on B deck. Sally had their cabin. But it was on A deck that Conchita said she had seen Mario with his partner. It was on A deck according to Mrs Fairbrother that Sir John Meadows had seen Conchita with Mario, and Max Bernstein had seen the bridge-playing gang. Whatever had been done to Felicity had been done here where he was standing. Or hereabouts. And some damage perhaps had been done to the rail; something that a lick of paint could restore, at any rate could cover up.

Such as what? Such as a rope with a weight on it? A soft thing like a rope? It would break with much of a weight on it. Or no, that would not apply to a heavy rope, a nylon rope, such as climbers use, or a *wire* rope.

Conchita had said Mario and the girl were together and then he had thrown her overboard and come away alone. A swift blow in that struggle and, to make sure the body reached its destination, lower it on a line until the water took it and swept it away. No trace then except

he slight chafing of the rail. *Which the Captain had
rdered to be painted out the next morning.*

Why? Who had reported it to him? How was it the
ermudan police had not investigated? What was the
neaning of this conspiracy of silence on the part of
rowthorne and his officers, for more than two others
ust surely be involved. And then to leave the Wet Paint
oard there, carelessly ignored for so many days, its
nessage turned, out of sight to passengers. Whose care-
essness was that?

He thought over his own dealings with the Captain in
ne light of the information he had brought back on
oard after his visit ashore at Bridgetown. His researches
nere had not been questioned or criticised. No dis-
pproval at all. Full understanding over Conchita. She
ad been restored to her job on the old terms. As far
s he knew there had been no trouble with the other
wo stewardesses. The one on A deck was like an old-
ashioned lady's maid, or what he imagined an old-
ashioned lady's maid must have been like. Tim had very
ague ideas about domestic servants, who had played
 limited part in his early childhood's home and dis-
ppeared from it entirely in 1942, when he was five
ears old. The stewardess on C deck was far more con-
emporary. Perhaps he ought to have made their
cquaintance and learned more from them about Con-
hita. But he had a feeling they would be less than
o-operative.

Turning away from the rail Tim went back to his
abin. The pencil and paper lay where he had left them.
ut now he had something to write down. Using his
ersonal shorthand he scribbled for several minutes, then
at back, slowly crumpling the paper into a ball. It was
ll nonsense. A vision of Mario rose before him, going
p to one of the crew to borrow a rope—"Rope, sir?
Vhat kind of rope?"

"Not too stiff to handle. Wire, preferably: more likely
o scratch the paint."

153

"This do, sir?"

"Fine. I'll see you have it back. I only want it to lower my wife's body into the sea."

Rot. Obvious rot. The ravings of a nut. He must b half-way round the bend already.

With despair in his heart, for in spite of demolishing his latest theory, Tim still felt he was somehow near enlightenment, he set out to find comfort from Sally.

She was not on deck. Nor was Mrs Fairbrother. On the other hand there were some newcomers who bowed stiffly as he passed. He went along the corridor to Sally's cabin and knocked. Her voice said 'Come in' so he knocked again. Her voice said from just inside, "Who is it?"

"Tim."

"Oh."

The door opened, let him in and was shut quickly behind him. Sally, who had been dozing on her bunk, greeted him with a very welcoming smile and an insincere apology for her state of undress.

"Rot. There's absolutely no difference between this rig and a bikini, except that the lower bit comes up rather higher and covers more tummy."

"And both bits, as you call them, are transparent."

"So what? I love you, Sally."

Though his arms were round her and she knew he spoke truly she stalled for the simple pleasure of it, asking, "Was that why you've come? To tell me?"

"No. I've forgotten why I came. I love you. Don't talk I love you."

A good deal later Tim was lying on his back on Sally's bunk, staring at the ceiling and listening to Sally running the shower. He was staring at the marks he had noticed there before and gradually the idea that had nagged at him for so long before Sally swept it away, came back more forcefully than ever. He sprang up. The shower was still running, she would not hear if he spoke, if he shouted others might hear. He tried the bathroom door

154

She had not locked it but she had pulled the plastic curtains round the shower. Smiling at this access of modesty he said, "The bar at six, my darling," and retreated before she had time to answer.

On B deck he found what he sought. He went down to his cabin to work out the next move. Punctually at six, sitting in the bar lounge with a radiant Sally he said, "I never told you what I came to you about this afternoon."

"No," she answered. "Go on. Tell me now."

"I can't now. Or not just yet. But I will. Only—"

"Well?"

Her present gentleness touched him deeply. He felt for her knee under the table.

"If I disappear for a bit after dinner you won't think—"

"You've deserted me after having your way etcetera. No, darling. I won't think anything. It won't be dangerous, will it?"

"Definitely not. No more melodrama. I promise."

So when, suddenly leaving his coffee untouched, Tim muttered a quick excuse and followed the cadet officer out of the dining saloon Sally continued her conversation as if she had not noticed his withdrawal.

Tim caught up Dick Groves in the corridor.

"Can I have a word?" he asked in a low voice, for the junior wireless officer was just ahead of them.

"Why yes, of course."

"Outside on B deck," said Tim firmly.

He led the way to the spot where the fresh lick of paint on the rail showed so plainly.

"I want you to tell me why the rail has been re-painted just here and also in a similar position only a trifle further forward on the rail above."

Dick stared, then said with a short laugh, "Because the skipper is very particular about scratches to his paint."

"Scratches? There *were scratches?*"

Becoming obviously uncomfortable Dick muttered, "I

suppose so. That's the normal reason for touching up, isn't it?"

"I don't believe the reason here was normal," Tim said. "Far from it." He pointed upwards. "And those marks, that were overlooked, I imagine. Would you call them normal?"

"Which marks?" Dick asked in his turn. "You're imagining things."

"I don't think so. There are similar marks in Sally Combes's cabin. We both noticed them days ago. I have only just realised what they must mean."

There was silence between them for several seconds. Then Dick Groves said, in a very different tone of voice, "I think you ought to speak to Captain Crowthorne. I think he would be interested."

"Oh yes?"

"Before you get in touch with anyone else with these —er—ideas."

"O.K." Tim said. He saw that Dick had now blocked his retreat along the corridor, but the way was open to the iron staircase leading to the bridge. "Carry on," he said, leaning back against the rail to let the other pass in front.

"After you," Dick said and as they moved away, with Tim in front he added, "and don't try any funny business, will you? The Old Man is a great one for discipline, as you may have gathered."

"Just one thing," Tim said, pausing to look round. "On that night the ship was rollng. Am I right?"

"Rolling!" Dick laughed. "The understatement of the cruise."

They continued, both silent, towards the bridge.

CHAPTER XV

Selena left Nassau very early the next morning. None of the passengers bothered to get up to see her leave. Those who had been on the cruise from the start had seen as many sailings as they wanted; the newcomers were not cruising but going home. Their chief interest was in getting there.

Tim and Sally kept to their respective cabins. After the many and varied excitements of the last two days they were exhausted. Both slept soundly and dreamlessly and woke at sea feeling thankful there would be a quiet interval before the next perhaps unwelcome upheaval.

For Tim this meant the final resolution of his problems, professional and personal; for Sally the need to introduce him at once to her uncle and aunt and announce their engagement.

She was glad there would be a waiting time of a few days while her flight back to England was arranged. Tim wanted them to fly on the same plane and he too had matters to clear up with the local newspaper. His own mother, a widow, was living in Italy with friends of her late husband. There was no need for him to get in touch with her at once. He had not seen her for three years: they corresponded very seldom.

Sally wrote a long explanatory letter to her father which she proposed to send at once when she landed. Following a much less personal one to her mother, written at Nassau the evening they got there and describing the police actions against the gang, she realised there would be some shock at home as well as surprise. But her father was the more likely of the two to take it all quietly.

There was now a different atmosphere on the ship,

particularly among those passengers who had begun the cruise at Southampton and intended to finish it there. They had been promised a quiet enjoyable period of rest, sunshine and pleasant companionship. Instead of this the first part of the trip had been cold and rough and after a brief period south of the Azores, when the poster promise had been equalled if not excelled, they had entered upon a series of violent happenings that made them feel they had been used as extras in a more than usually extravagant crime film.

Well, that was over now, Mrs Fairbrother explained hopefully to her little circle, gathered as so often in the chairs near the swimming pool, enjoying the morning sunshine, now on the starboard side of *Selena*.

"I certainly hope you're right," Mrs Newbuckle said. "If I thought there'd be a repetition I'd persuade Fred to let us go straight home from Bermuda."

"Don't do that," Mrs Fairbrother pleaded.

"No, you mustn't," Lady Meadows echoed, looking at her husband, who only grunted non-committally and began to struggle up from his seat.

"Only another little walk," he explained, waving his wife back. "Missed my daily mile with all that schimozzle at Nassau."

He stumped away and presently joined the Bernsteins who were on the foredeck, looking at some large yellow patches of Sargasso weed floating all round the ship.

"It makes a change from flying fish," Sir John said.

"They were always so beautiful," Max sighed.

"But I wish they would not serve them for the lunch," Lottie complained gently. "It is not the very good taste, is it? Not like our northern herring. Besides, I see it on the menu and I think of this so beautiful sight—like —like—"

"Kingfishers darting over a stream," said Sir John unexpectedly. "If you get the sun on them at the right angle. Not bright enough otherwise."

"Kingfisher?" asked Mr Bernstein.

"Small bird," Sir John held his hands near together to show the size. "Very bright blue and green plumage. Fairly common near smallish streams, rivers and so on. I've seen them often fishing for trout."

"Kingfisher," Mr Bernstein repeated. "This bird eats the fishes also?"

"That's the idea. At least I think it's mostly flies and other insects. Perhaps they might pick up very small fry in the shallows. I really don't know."

They were all silent, then Mrs Bernstein said, "Your wife is not with you. Lady Meadows is well, I hope?"

"Quite well, thank you. She's on deck, back there, chatting. She was a bit knocked up by Nassau. Nasty business. Can't think why the police had to chase those beggars all over the ship. They should have sent some plain clothes chaps to pick them up as they went ashore."

Max Bernstein sighed.

"In England, yes. I think impossible here. They would all have escaped into the skier's speed boat. Or else hidden on the ship."

"Like the last one young Rogers nabbed. Good work, that."

"He had, isn't it, the tip-off from Conchita," Mrs Bernstein said. "Mrs Fairbrother told me."

The men exchanged smiles.

"Conchita is still on board," added Mrs Bernstein.

"Lottie," warned her husband. "No more longings for excitements. You say you want to know exactly and then you terrify."

Sir John turned from the rail to continue his walk.

"I must say I'm inclined to agree with Mrs Bernstein," he said before he left them. "Conchita has been sacked I believe—finally, this time. So Crowthorne told me and I didn't think it was meant to be in confidence. He was blazing over the hidden crook and that woman had something to do with hiding him, even if she did warn Rogers. She's going for good at Bermuda."

"Then we shall never know if she killed Mrs Fennister

159

or not, shall we, Max?"

"We might," he said and murmured to the yellow weed, "if we don't know already."

"What's that you say, Max?"

"Nothing of importance," he answered.

Sir John on his way back met Tim going towards the swimming pool to bathe. They exchanged greetings and as the older man seemed inclined to talk Tim slowed his steps to walk beside him.

"Did you manage to get your various stories off in Nassau in time?" Sir John asked.

"Various?"

"Well, yes. The crooks I suppose was the most important. But the Fennister drowning and the stewardess. Not to mention your—illness."

"As a matter of fact, sir," Tim said, "it was really all part of the same story. At least, it was two stories that got mixed up together."

"Indeed. I had a small part in it, in both stories, I may say. But you know that, since you came to warn me."

"Yes, indeed. I know a good deal more now than I did then."

"*Do* you?"

Sir John stopped, amazed, indignant. These journalists! Then *how?* His mind rushed to the new snooping devices, wire-tapping, bugging, tiny tape recorders, everything he found at home in the thrillers he reserved for the week-end.

"Very easy, sir," Tim said, wishing he had not gone so far. "Mrs Fairbrother overheard you and the Bernsteins in the writing room and—"

"That woman!" Sir John began, then laughed. "Our own fault," he went on. "Public place. Those writing tables are perfect screens. Besides, everyone goes to her for news. We do ourselves. My wife's there now."

They had almost arrived, so Tim left Sir John and moved forward more quickly, hearing, as he went down

160

the steps to the pool, Lady Meadows say to her husband, "John, Mrs Fairbrother says Conchita swears those men murdered Mrs Fennister because she refused to pay them blackmail."

"Blackmail? How could—"

"Conchita swears Mario Fennister is really her husband."

Sir John was astonished.

"Then why didn't she claim him at Bermuda and denounce the crooks?"

Mrs Fairbrother said, "At that time Conchita was afraid Mario would be accused. Or even herself. They were all there on the deck at some time that night."

"And were seen, as you know," Sir John said gravely.

Not at all put out Mrs Fairbrother said, "I told Conchita that. She did not mind. She knew already. I think Sally must have told her. But she did mind Tim coming on board."

"Why?"

Damn it, Tim thought, straining to hear the full extent of Mrs Fairbrother's knowledge. The woman's a human sponge, he thought, a piece of blotting paper, a computer of a deadly kind. He dived, with force, quite near the side of the pool so that the water splashed up and over the screened rail. With satisfaction he heard little cries of distress from beyond it. He swam away quickly and as Sir John appeared at the top of the steps ducked under water and stayed there while his breath lasted. When he came up again puffing Sir John had gone.

But his dive had broken off the talk about Conchita. Lady Meadows got up and went away with Sir John. The Newbuckles decided they had had enough sun and would seek the shade to cool off before lunch. Mrs Fairbrother was left alone. Sighing contentedly she pulled her book out of her bag and began to read.

When Tim came out to find his towel she lifted her eyes and said, "You needn't have half drowned us, Tim. I wouldn't have given you away."

"Wouldn't you? Really and truly?"

"Really and truly. I respect your profession."

Wrapping himself in his towel he sat on the deck at her feet.

"Now why did you say that, I wonder?"

"Because—you may not believe me—about forty years ago I was a journalist myself."

Tim gaped. He was beyond speech.

"And that's something you are to keep to yourself," she said. "At present. When you get home you may tell Sally."

"Yes, mam," Tim said in a very subdued voice.

Talking it over with Sally later that day they decided that though the fact of Mrs Fairbrother's early profession did account for her observation and her shrewd guesses it did not cover her very frequent indiscretions.

"What about yours?" Sally said to tease him. "You began by confiding in me that she made you promise to tell no one."

"We must never have secrets from one another," Tim said with a theatrical gesture.

"Granted. Of course Mrs F would allow for you telling me. Oh well, I don't gossip." She smiled at him. "There isn't anyone now I'd want to gossip with."

"Added to which," Tim said, "I don't mind betting our Mrs F has already spread the news of Conchita's claim on Mario to anyone likely to be interested. It was my connection with it I didn't want her to give away so widely."

"Then I hope you didn't sprinkle her too seriously. It would never do to give her pneumonia. I daren't think what deadly secrets she might babble to Dr McRae in her delirium."

"Idiot," Tim said tenderly.

Mrs Longford, equally exhausted by the Nassau excitements, kept to her cabin, except at meal times, for two days after leaving the Bahamas. On the third day she intercepted Captain Crowthorne on his rounds. He

162

too was feeling the strain of his position and did not hesitate to tell her so.

"Not now, Ann. You don't seem to realise what people are saying about you."

"Oh, don't I? And about you too, Jack."

He frowned but did not answer.

"I only want to make sure what will happen at Bermuda. Why didn't you get rid of that woman at Nassau?"

"Conchita? Stupid bitch! I would have too, only it'd have been murder. I couldn't shove her off to have her throat cut in the next twelve hours."

"Were there so many more of them?"

"How do I know? The cops told me our four were only the tip of the iceberg—of several icebergs—operating all over the area. Headquarters in a Central American state."

"Which one?"

He looked at her steadily, with cold anger.

"Seeing what your future plans are you'd better not know. Besides, they may just have been putting me off firing her. They didn't want her in their manor."

She shook her head at him.

"Don't spoil it now, Jack. Not after all we've been through together."

Captain Crowthorne turned sharply and walked away from her.

So, very quietly, in flat seas and perpetual sunshine, in a routine of comfort that was secretly beginning to pall for the all-rounders on the cruise, *Selena* moved over the Atlantic and at last into harbour again at Bermuda, where about fifteen of her passengers, among them Sally and Tim, prepared to disembark.

Sally was up early, fastening her two suitcases and stacking them ready to be taken out by the cabin steward. She had gone her rounds with the expected tips the night before, totally exhausting her purse. But asking for Conchita she found that the stewardess was leaving too and was finally off duty.

Having dealt with her bags Sally decided to say good-bye to Mrs Fairbrother. The latter had already asked for her home address. Though Sally would be back in England many days before the old lady she had no doubt they would meet again. Mrs Fairbrother lived in Hampstead; Tim would be working in London. It might be fun to keep up with this retired, but not at all retiring, member of his profession.

Mrs Fairbrother was not in her cabin. She was sitting on one of the more comfortable seats near the Purser's desk. Sally did not see her at once for the number of people who were standing about and moving to and fro hid her from view. But Mrs Fairbrother saw Sally and called out to her.

"I went to your cabin," the girl said, "to say goodbye and thank you for being so kind to me."

"Nice child," Mrs Fairbrother said, holding up her face to be kissed. "I shall insist upon you and Tim coming to see me at home."

Sally, still bending over her, promised to do this.

"Have you said goodbye to everyone?" Mrs Fairbrother asked.

"Nearly. I couldn't find Conchita. I asked for her and then remembered. But I might run into her on shore. She's leaving. I expect you know."

"She hopes to find Mario and claim him. If he has left she will follow. Or so she told me."

"Why do we—well, go on trying—"

"To help her? To watch her? Knowing she is very dangerous, a liar, a potential murderess? Perhaps for that reason. You know," Mrs Fairbrother said, "to my way of thinking we are all making too much of a mystery of Conchita. I believe the whole thing has been a very simple story"

"You said that before. How?" Sally asked. "I don't get."

"You'll see," Mrs Fairbrother assured her.

Sally, with Tim at her side, stood near the head of

the gangway while it was being fixed in position. They had already taken leave of Captain Crowthorne and the other principal officers. All the luggage, the Purser had told them, would be taken direct to the Customs shed by the port authorities' own staff. There were only sixteen passengers leaving.

"I thought it was fifteen," Sally whispered to Tim.

"Hush."

"I expect they didn't count Conchita."

"I said hush. She's just behind us."

Sure enough, there was Conchita, dressed in all her finery as she had been at Bridgetown. Her eyes were shining, her olive cheeks were flushed, her mouth a little open, white teeth showing. Sally moved a little closer to Tim. She looked down at the quayside.

Uncle Oswald was there with Aunt Hilda, standing near a uniformed man who seemed to be with a picturesque figure in peon costume, breeches, yellow shirt, boots and spurs, with a sombrero fastened under his chin by a leather strap and pulled down over his face.

Then, as the word was given to start and the seaman at the head of the gangway stepped aside and the passengers began moving down a small commotion in the doorway behind made all heads turn.

The Captain came out, Mrs Longford came out and between them, to Sally's astonishment, a second, a younger, slimmer Mrs Longford, smiling, expectant, her very short white mini-skirt swinging, her feet in close-fitting, soft white circus shoes, moving in absolute control.

At that moment Conchita, whose eyes had been raking the crowd gathered below the gangway cried aloud in Spanish, "Mario! Praise be to God, Mario!"

Sally and Tim heard her. They stared down, searching the gathered knot of people and saw a shortish, sturdy man in white slacks and a thin white vest that showed off his powerful shoulders step forward, look upward, wave—but not at Conchita.

Sally was pushed violently to one side. Tim yelled a

warning. Conchita plunged to the gangway, a two-edged knife in her hand.

The man below clapped twice. The girl after one backward look sprang forward, not down the steps of the gangway but up to its rail, along which she ran or rather seemed to float, to the angle where its second half turned off to reach the wharf. The man clapped again twice. The girl leaped, turned in the air and dived, her hands outstretched to his. He caught her hands, threw her up, so that she turned in the air and landed with her feet on his shoulders, her back to the ship. He clapped for the third time and she turned a back somersault over his head to land on the ground facing him, holding his supporting hands. He leaned forward and kissed her.

An immediate uproar broke out. Shouts of applause, wild clapping, cries of "Felicity! Felicity!" Unnoticed hitherto, most of the ship's crew, not only those issued with white uniform, were lining the rail on the fore-deck. Most of them had at one time or another caught a glimpse of practice on the top deck. Now they had seen a real act. And was it good!

The passengers who had known her were frantic with joy. Those who had only heard the story, the mystery, the rumours and half-truths, shouted their appreciation of a wholly delightful climax. No tragedy. No murder. A hoax, of course! What a brilliant idea for an advertisement! What skill! What daring! No practice possible for them, of course. Or had they?

Most of the onlookers had not seen the knife. None of them remembered Conchita, except those who had been caught into the net of her story. Mrs Longford had tried to rush into the woman's path when Felicity moved forward to the gangway, but Captain Crowthorne held her. A seaman at the gangway and other officers were held back by the passengers surging forward. But Tim had followed his cry by pushing in Conchita's wake and Sally kept behind him. They found her lying sprawled on her face, sobbing her heart out, the knife

166

still clutched in her hand. She had tripped on the second step when Felicity sailed up to the rail out of her reach.

Tim stopped dead, not at sight of the knife but of the man dressed as a peon, sombrero now slipping to the back of his neck, helping his upward run with both hands on the rails of the gangway. He had been dressed like this in Bridgetown. Tim drew a deep breath of recognition and waited.

The man reached the prostrate figure, bent and took the knife, with the other hand picked Conchita up by the clothes on her back, set her on her feet and spoke a few growling words in a dialect no one near them understood.

Conchita stared. Her face was sullen, her cheeks fallen. She looked old and tired.

"So. It is you, Ambrosan," she said in Spanish. "Now it is all over. It is finished."

She made no resistance while he straightened her clothes with both hands, holding the knife between his teeth. Then, taking it back into one hand he put the other round her waist and led her down to the wharf.

No one tried to stop them. The police chief made a signal with his hand to let them pass. The man paused a moment near the Customs shed to take Conchita's bag that a young negro porter was guarding there. He gave the boy a coin; polite words were exchanged.

The pair went on their way, walking slowly, but upright, with dignity, the man's arm still about her. Behind them the shouting and the clapping for the talented Fenestri pair still continued. The two white-clad figures bowed and curtseyed and waved their amused acknowledgement again and again and again.

CHAPTER XVI

"Ambrosan is her first husband," Tim explained. "Her only legal one."

"Which makes Mario's supposed bigamy null and void," said Aunt Hilda.

"His marriage to Felicity is legal, would be a nicer way of putting it," said Uncle Oswald.

"You'd better explain, Tim," Sally urged.

The four of them were sitting relaxed and very comfortable on the verandah of Uncle Oswald's house. The garden lay in front of them, an English garden, landscaped, green, carefully tended and watered, a profusion of flowers including many that would never be found in England.

Sally, to whom these surroundings were familiar, found herself wondering if the events of the last two weeks were real, so dreamlike did they seem now that they were finally behind her. Tim, on the other hand, after his long self-imposed exile in foreign lands, was quite bewildered by this sudden return to an atmosphere and surroundings that had for long passed from reality into his dreams. He roused himself with an effort.

"It began in Bridgetown," he said.

"I thought you went on board here, on purpose to get Conchita's story," Sally interrupted.

"So I did. At least, until I saw and recognised her it was the Fennister story I was after."

Uncle Oswald said, "Shut up, Sally. Let Tim tell it his own way."

"Thank you. I will."

Tim began again.

"Having recognised Conchita in spite of her uniform

as a stewardess, I naturally suspected some very dirty work in Felicity's disappearance and decided to watch her whenever possible. That was how I first began to know Sally, apart from the fact that I was put next to her for meals."

"He has a passion for ulterior motives," Sally said.

"I didn't get very far at first. Sally and Mrs Fairbrother were helpful to a limited, a very limited, extent. I'll tell you about that later. As I began by saying, it was at Bridgetown a real light came. Ambrosan."

"I wouldn't call him exactly a *light*," Sally criticised. "More a blob of darkness. I've never seen such perfectly black eyes and hair and that black drooping moustache . . ." She shuddered.

"Poor old Ambrosan," Tim countered. "I must say I felt sorry for him. You see, he came face to face with Conchita in the street when she was tripping along, all dolled up, going to meet Mario—as she thought. She let out one squawk, turned round and ran."

"I saw her arriving back on the ship," Sally explained. "She was still running, on her bare feet, holding her high-heeled sandals in one hand. Fantastic."

"I can imagine it," said Aunt Hilda, on a sympathetic note. "Poor woman, what a shock!"

"Poor old Ambrosan," Tim corrected. "She was the last person he expected to meet in the street. But from that moment he never let go."

Uncle Oswald asked mildly, "Did he accost you or did you nail him?"

Tim laughed.

"A bit of both, really. I was not far behind Conchita, hoping to see the meeting between her and Mario and draw my own conclusions about them. When she yelled and scarpered I must have looked astonished, which I was. The next minute Ambrosan had me by the arm shaking me and asking me in very bad Spanish who she was, was she called Conchita, how come I knew her and plenty more questions of the same sort. So I agreed I knew her and suggested we go and find a drink and exchange information. Which we did."

"It must have been an exciting moment for you," Sally said grudgingly. "And to think you never told me a word of it."

"Have a heart," Tim expostulated. "And you in old Fairbrother's pocket. I should think Conchita would have cut *all* our throats."

Aunt Hilda said, "Do stop interrupting, Sally. Tim, tell us what Ambrosan had to say."

"First of all that he married Conchita way back some twenty years ago in their own country. They had three children that survived, two others that died young. No doctors where they were living. Ambrosan was a cattle man on a ranch. Out in the wild most of the time. Conchita was about sixteen, he thinks, when he married her."

"A real legal marriage?" asked Uncle Oswald.

"Quite legal. Catholic. He still had his marriage papers, in a small flat leather bag on a string round his neck. He showed me. When he did that I told him I had met Conchita in Brazil, when she was a dancer in cabaret and had been deserted by Mario whom she described as her husband."

"That shook him, I suppose?" Sally could not help saying.

"Profoundly. I told him everything Conchita had said about going to Europe and so on. I also told him I had afterwards checked this marriage which appeared to be authentic. Conchita had done quite a job of fancy lying. Ambrosan said gloomily she had always been a prize liar. I did not doubt it."

"So then?" they all asked as Tim sat back, brooding on Ambrosan's wrongs.

"Well, he told me of his struggles to bring up his family of small children without Conchita. But not, I gathered, altogether without female help. How they were now self-supporting and he was free to follow his own desire, which was to find Conchita. He told me he had seen a picture of her in a newspaper showing her as a dancer, and had dug out the manager of the troupe she was with and so traced her along to the cabaret in Brazil and at last to her new job on *Selena*. He was actually on his way to the ship when he ran into her. He told me he was so surprised at the change in her—he hadn't seen her for so many years—that he failed to catch hold of her before she ran off."

Again Tim stopped speaking. Uncle Oswald leaned across to renew his brandy while Aunt Hilda filled his coffee cup.

"I suppose you told him Conchita had fired herself from the ship because she expected to meet Mario, whom she regarded as her husband?" Sally suggested.

"I told him that. She thought Mario would be in Bridgetown. It was difficult to know what more to tell him. He was following *Selena*'s movements carefully, so he had read about the Fennister disaster—supposed disaster —in the late edition of the morning paper. This had not affected him much, as it had no significance for him at that time. Even after I told him, he thought naïvely that it eliminated Mario. Of course it had removed the acrobat from the ship. He didn't know the pair, with Mrs Longford, were leaving anyway. His concern was always, and solely, for Conchita."

"He still loved her?" Aunt Hilda asked, incredulous.

"No. I don't think so. But he had to get her back. Her desertion was an intolerable insult."

"That was what *she* said!" Sally cried. "About Mario."

But no one was listening. Tim went on.

"It was a very tricky situation for me. The last thing I wanted was for Ambrosan to go storming on board after Conchita, creating a scandal and all my fault. Captain Crowthorne would have been livid and rightly so. In the end I told Ambrosan she had left the ship, taking her belongings with her and was looking for Mario, who, I reminded him, had promised to meet her there in Bridgetown after he'd cleared up the business

of his wife's death. Felicity's death. I gave him the detail
of his second marriage to this girl. Ambrosan though
this very funny. He laughed till he cried. He cried quite
a lot after that, from grief and uncertainty. We'd been
drinking steadily. At least he had. He was pretty high
by then."

"So he stayed in Barbados," Uncle Oswald said slowly
"And *Selena* sailed away with Conchita and without
you. Why?"

Tim looked uncomfortable.

"It took me longer than I intended to get rid of Am
brosan. I missed the boat—literally. So I found a cheap
hotel in Bridgetown and made some very expensive calls
—to my editor and to Mario. I got an interesting piece
of news from Mario. He swore he'd never intended to go
to Barbados. I told him Conchita claimed to be his
wife and expected to find him there. He said Felicity had
been his wife and it was inhuman of me to make these
suggestions. He rang off."

"Good for Mario!" said Sally.

"Not so good," Tim answered. "I was going to put
him wise about Ambrosan, but he didn't give me a
chance. However, I knew *Selena* would be in Port of
Spain the next day so I arranged to fly there early and
rejoin the ship."

"So you couldn't have been waiting on the quay," Sally
said. "Mrs Longford was just stringing me along, the
bitch."

"Mrs Longford wanted to find out how much you
knew," Tim told her. "And how well we were getting
along together. If you'd known how to handle those
binoculars—"

"Had you forgotten?" Uncle Oswald said mildly. "I
showed you several times, Sally."

She hung her head. Aunt Hilda hastened to say, "I'm
never much good with them, Sally. Oswald hasn't the
patience to teach anyone anything."

"Abominable libel!" her husband protested.

To check this rudimentary family quarrel Tim went on. "You see, I had to know what they were all doing. I mean Mario, Conchita and Ambrosan. I had to know when that particular balloon would go up. Mario was at the greatest disadvantage, because he didn't know of Ambrosan's existence. Well, Conchita went ashore at Port of Spain and neither Ambrosan nor Mario showed up there. It must have been about then that Conchita became really frightened for Mario. She genuinely believed he had got rid of his wife for her sake. At least—"

"Oh, I think it was genuine," Sally agreed. "But confused."

"When I went back to *Selena*," Tim continued, "I spoke to Captain Crowthorne and explained my position and gave him the facts about Conchita and her two husbands. He seemed more relieved than I expected; much more cordial. I thought I was in for a rocket but he gave me a whisky instead. It was later on he began to think I was a real trouble maker. But that wasn't my fault at all. I never expected that set of thugs to make real trouble until they took it into their heads to eliminate me."

Tim explained his part in the events that followed.

"We've had it in the papers," Uncle Oswald said. "You're quite famous here, you know, Tim."

"Then the sooner we get our flight fixed the better," he answered.

"Don't be too modest," Aunt Hilda said. "I'm sure we're all most grateful for the way you've—well—looked after Sally."

The engaged couple exchanged a quick glance.

"And we're very proud we're going to have you in the family," she concluded. "Aren't we, Oswald?"

Uncle Oswald gave a suitably British, unidentifiable grunt.

As no one else seemed inclined to speak Aunt Hilda went on bravely, "Now tell us about the Fennisters, Tim. This Ann Longford is Felicity's elder sister. Both of them knew the Crowthornes in England. That is why they were travelling in Jack Crowthorne's ship. I suppose that explains why he was willing to carry through the deception, I do hope he doesn't get into trouble with his owners."

"Probably not," Tim answered. "It was bad luck on him. He knew what was going to happen. He'd agreed to hide Felicity for a couple of days. The plan was for Mario to tell Conchita to leave the ship in Bridgetown and meet him there. *Selena* would sail without her, he would fly to Port of Spain, pick up Felicity and Mrs Longford and fly on to their first stand in South America. All that had to be altered after Conchita came back to the ship and I told Crowthorne about Ambrosan. The Captain radioed the news back to Bermuda, and Mario stayed put. The girls had to stay on board with the chance of Felicity being discovered getting more likely every day. No wonder Crowthorne's temper deteriorated as time went by."

"I should think the thugs breaking into criminal action must have been a blessing in disguise for him," said Uncle Oswald.

"Rather a heavy disguise," Sally said ruefully. "I never want . . ."

"Don't brood on it, my dear," Aunt Hilda said kindly.

"And all that time you were still trying to find out how Felicity had been disposed of," Uncle Oswald chuckled. "Crowthorne never even hinted?"

"We got some leads we needed," Tim explained. "For instance, Sally saw a woman on the bridge—it must have been Felicity taking the air—when she dashed off for help for me."

"A glimpse only. I thought it was Mrs Longford," Sally defended herself. "I was really thinking most about Tim —panicking, actually."

"Of course, my darling. Bless you," Tim said, smiling at her.

"Tell us how you finally worked out she was alive and

on the ship," Uncle Oswald suggested.

"It was simple, really. If we discarded suicide, which seemed ridiculous, and eliminated Mario and Conchita *and* the gang, there was only one answer—that she was still alive."

"You found you could make all those eliminations?"

"Why, yes. Mario wouldn't kill his act. Felicity didn't give a damn for his earlier marriage. Conchita is vicious, but she was afraid. It was when the thug I sat on said 'The other one laughed, too' I got the idea clearly. After that it was a question of finding evidence."

"And you succeeded?"

"I found, when I looked, that repairs had been made to the paint of the rail on both decks, A and B, almost directly one above the other. This suggested scratches from a rope or wire attached to something heavy swinging backwards and forwards. I remembered Conchita's confession that she thought she had seen Mario throw Felicity over the rail. We thought she must be lying, but I believe now that she did see this. There was a very heavy swell that night. When the ship rolled to port the side they were all on, anything heavy on a line thrown from the rail of A deck would be swung well clear of the vessel's side. The next roll to starboard would bring the object in again, well in. If the timing and the length of the line used were right the object would land on B deck below, just above the rail."

"It sounds possible, but crazy," said Uncle Oswald, but he was smiling and his eyes were very bright.

"It was quite possible to that pair. The girl is exceptional. They work together automatically. You saw the exhibition this morning. It was unexpected, unrehearsed. But most beautifully done."

"I should say!" cried Sally. "Felicity took one look behind when Tim called out to warn her and immediately did the obvious thing to her; she jumped on the rail of the gangway and ran out of reach along it. Mario reacted at once when he saw her do this. He directed the rest of the action, probably one of the routines they do or something very like. Their timing was perfect, their combined understanding miraculous. Didn't you think so?" she asked, turning to Aunt Hilda.

"Indeed, yes. I must say I concluded it was all put on for advertisement, but if you say it was spontaneous then indeed it was miraculous."

This concluded the discussion, rather to Tim's relief. He was ready to put all of the past behind him now. There was plenty of work to be done planning the future, both in the immediate sense and in that more distant time when Sally and he would join forces in the search for happiness. On past form he was inclined to be cautious, even to issue private warnings to himself. But his defences were crumbling fast and he knew it.

This belief was upheld the next day when Sally insisted upon showing him the pleasures of Bermuda, swimming and sailing. He followed willingly and with contentment where she and her relations led, finally in a very openly engineered talk with Aunt Hilda, sitting on the sand watching Sally and her uncle surfing happily for the last time before going home for dinner.

"So you're off back to England tomorrow," Aunt Hilda said. "Does that please you?"

"Yes. I'll be glad to be back. I don't regret these three years away. But . . . well. . . ." He laughed, looking away and said, "Sally."

Aunt Hilda agreed. She was sympathetic, she probed gently, but mercilessly. In his present mood Tim was defenceless, so he did not resent it. As he told Sally later, "She knows more about me now than you've started to ask, my love."

"Such as?"

"That I'm not what she would call well-connected, but I'm reasonably well educated and civilised. That I have made a few valuable friends over the years, some of whom your uncle and she know, or at any rate their fathers and mothers. That she thinks we are very well suited."

"Big of her," said Sally, inclined to be annoyed at this. "That she thinks I ought to be able to support you in due course, but I must let you go on working for a bit."

"Well, really! Did she tell you Uncle Oswald has already practically fixed a new job for me on the strength of my work for him?"

"No, she did not. Nor have you, for that matter."

She was all contrition.

"I'm sorry. He didn't tell me himself till this morning. Damn Aunt Hilda! Is she trying to break us up with her snooty ideas. My people might be difficult. But not these two— At least, I hoped not."

He kissed her and felt an added confidence.

"We'll be all right. The main thing is not to get into futile tangles, like the ghastly couples on radio and TV who do nothing but misunderstand, suspect and needle each other in perfectly empty situations for perfectly bogus ends."

"I promise not to nag. I wouldn't dare."

"Afraid I'd run off back to South America?"

It had often been in her mind that he might not be able to settle anywhere for long. But she laughed and said, "I'd follow. Like Conchita." And more seriously, "I hope she'll find her children again to comfort her. And not run into the Fenestri act—ever."

"Mario and Co have left," Tim said. "This morning, for Rio."

"How d'you know?"

"I took the trouble to find out."

"And Conchita?"

"No news. But they thought that pair had left too. There was a freighter leaving today for Buenos Ayres."

"So that's all right," Sally said. "All the ends tied up and wonderful times ahead for us, my darling."

So be it, Tim thought, with a great uplift of feeling and of hope.

CHAPTER XVII

When the stirring scene on the wharf came to an end, when Mario and Felicity were at last released from the adulation of the crowd and allowed to join Ann Longford in the hired car where Mario's driver, who was also his dresser, sat waiting, a sad air of anti-climax descended. Workers returned to their work, *Selena*'s crew to their stations, her passengers to pursue the activities they had planned for the day.

All except the Bernsteins. In a revulsion of feeling Lottie demanded to finish the cruise on the ship. She was not to be turned from this wish, so Max had to retrieve their luggage and make the necessary rearrangements.

"But why, my dearest?" he asked many times during the afternoon. "Why, when we have seen a so happy reunion—two reunions—?"

"One happy, one—I shudder at."

"Conchita? She deserved a litle punishment, a little humiliation. Crowthorne has told me. That man was indeed her true husband. She ran from him in Barbados. It spoiled the plan to reunite Felicity and Mario in Trinidad."

"So!"

"Then why should we not take our plane and be at home tomorrow?"

"Because I cannot go ashore here. There will be rejoicings for the Fenestris and I do not wish to be involved in them. And that poor Conchita. She will be silent in misery. I do not wish to be where she is too."

"This is sentimental, Lottie. It is not worthy of you."

"It is what I feel. Be patient, Max. We will be able to have more games of bridge with the Meadows."

He made a face at her.

"And best of all we will listen to how Mrs Fairbrother explains the whole of these events to us, which she has known or discovered from the beginning."

"I do not think that is possible, even to Mrs Fairbrother."

So there were many who went ashore, eager to continue their excitement, though they were not clear how to do so. But some of the older passengers stayed on board. The veterans of the cruise, Mrs Fairbrother, the Meadowses, the Bernsteins and the Newbuckles gathered in a nearly empty lounge for tea and made plans to have a mild celebration that evening in honour of Captain Crowthorne's skill and courage during those most unusual hazards he had had to face since they left Southampton.

This demanded a visit to the Chief Steward and another to the head steward in the dining saloon. The Captain's table was rearranged to include the Newbuckles for that evening only, taking the places of Mrs Longford and Miss O'Shea, whose chair had not been filled after Trinidad.

"We shall be pleased to make this a permanency, sir," the steward told Fred Newbuckle.

"That's good of you. I'll have to consult my wife. She may not approve of deserting our present table companions."

"There is no one coming aboard, sir, of—of—"

"More consequence than us? With more right to promotion? Nice to hear it," Mr Newbuckle said, with a very hard straight look at the steward.

"You took me up wrong, sir," the latter said, refusing to be put in his place by an upstart manufacturer from the north. He was a Portsmouth man and had served in the Royal Navy in his youth. He said, reading from his list. "This would be the order of the Captain's table then, Sir John, would it?"

Sir John nodded uncomfortably, Mr Bernstein nodded gravely, they turned a puce-faced Fred Newbuckle from the steward and took him up to B deck. The steward muttered a few sentences about "old times" and the young table stewards, who had stood listening with bundles of cutlery in their hands, grinned and played little tunes on the forks they held.

Captain Crowthorne was touched by this encomium. He had been put in a damned awkward position, he said, but the danger to Felicity was real and he couldn't let down his wife who had recommended *Selena* to her cousin, Ann Longford.

"I'd never have done such a thing in the ordinary way, but police protection in these parts and in the Caribbean isn't exactly Scotland Yard. Besides, Mario was throwing a temperament twice nightly. The girl can control him. Well, you saw her act here. He calls the moves, but she has them worked out to a split second. Incredible. My worst headache was keeping my officers sufficiently in the picture not to put me in irons as insane and take over the ship. Or alternatively let the cat out of the bag before I'd got rid of Conchita first and then our cardsharpers and blackmailers."

"We shall send a round robin of admiration and thanks to your owners," Mrs Fairbrother announced. "That ought to dispose of any other comments that may get to them."

"Have there been any?" Captain Crowthorne asked anxiously.

"You bet," Fred Newbuckle assured him. "I heard one nasty piece of work letting off about abduction, among other crimes."

"Know who it was?" the Captain asked blandly.

"I couldn't put a name to him," Mr Newbuckle answered, with a glance at his wife. She shook her head.

Sir John changed the conversation with a slow deliberate inquiry about their probable sailing time and hoped-for arrival back at Southampton. Captain Crowthorne was delighted to oblige him. Looking round the empty and half-filled tables in the dining saloon he

180

wondered how many of the passengers were ashore and how many of the expected newcomers for the trip home had cancelled their passages on account of the news from Nassau.

He need not have worried. Most of his passengers were ashore, many of them joining in the spontaneous, warm-hearted rejoicings at Felicity's reappearance that sent a crowd to the hotel where she and Mario were to spend the night.

Felicity put on her white-sequined circus dress and Mario his sequined waistcoat and they appeared hand in hand on the balcony outside their hotel room five storeys up. They did a few simple tricks and the people roared. Downstairs their impresario, a long cigar in his mouth, was signing them up by telephone in three more important cities of South America. He had shed tears of joy in the hired car when he had Felicity once more safely under his wing. He shed no tears over the contracts; his little eyes shone brightly as he made notes of the terms in his pocket diary.

Selena sailed the next morning. The passengers dropped back into their old routines or settled down to develop new ones. For some days the swimming pool was in use, though the water grew steadily colder, until finally there were no takers and it was emptied and cleaned and the canvas covers put on.

About the same time the officers abandoned their tropical kit and reappeared in the blue uniforms they had worn in home waters. The passengers, too, began to add cardigans and jackets to their summer clothes until even this was not enough to defeat the increasing head winds, and slacks and sweaters appeared to cover up the brown skins.

In due course *Selena* found the steady westerlies and more shelter on the decks in which to enjoy the weak May sunshine as she ran before them.

By this time the thoughts of all were turned to the nearing shores of England, heralded as the days passed by the sight of an increasing number of ships on the horizon. As they moved into the Channel approaches they found vessels passing them much closer and at shorter intervals. The universal feeling of contentment that had settled over the ship after leaving Bermuda vanished, split by each individual care for the future and never to be retrieved except in memory.

But long before this state was reached, in the first days out when the newcomers were all agog to learn of *Selena*'s curious adventures, Mrs Fairbrother had her hour of triumph. For, with her vigorous tenacity, her lively wits, her sixth sense for the essence of the thing she had, after seeing Felicity restored and in action, put all the rest of her knowledge together and arrived, with far fewer facts to support her, but rather more insight, at the same conclusion as Tim had done. This being so, she needed confirmation. The older officers would stall. Of the younger men only Dick Groves was likely to listen to her. She had met him with Sally, he was pleasant to talk to, neither shy nor arrogant.

It was not easy to get hold of him. She could not stop him when he was on some errand from the bridge. She could not ask one of the seniors how to find him off duty. She had to wait and hope that one of the public entertainment evenings would find him in attendance.

This happened towards the end of the cruise, on the occasion of the last of the dances in the lounge. The young man had been disappointed by a girl sitting near Mrs Fairbrother, who was claimed by one of her own party a few seconds before Dick got there. The old lady saw her opportunity and took it.

"Mr Groves," she said, half rising from her chair, "I'm sure you deserve a few minutes' rest and I have wanted to talk to you ever since we left Bermuda."

Considerably surprised Dick sat down in the chair next to her.

"I'll come straight to the point," she said. "There was no time to hear the whole story from Tim Rogers, but he gave me the outline and told me to ask you for the rest."

"The outline? What outline?" Dick stalled because he was most unwilling to talk about what to him was a strange, unpleasant episode that was best forgotten.

"You know perfectly well," Mrs Fairbrother said, smiling encouragement to hide her annoyance. "Not all the obvious details that we worked out step by step as it happened. Simply the way Conchita was tricked into believing Mario had thrown Felicity overboard. As I said, Tim hadn't time to tell me, but he thought you would do so."

"I'm not sure that I ought to," Dick said. "Captain Crowthorne—"

"Bother Captain Crowthorne!" Mrs Fairbrother cried. "It's all over and done with, but I go on puzzling and puzzling. At my age that is very bad for me."

Her eyes were so bright and her manner so vigorous that Dick knew this for the lie it was. His inclination was to excuse himself politely and leave her, but as he remembered that singular night and its sequel he found himself beginning to tell his account of it and once started he was unable to stop.

"We had been warned to keep an eye on Conchita and look out for developments. I don't know if any of the passengers were aware of the fact that the Fenestri pair practised on the upper deck regularly every day of the voyage."

"No, we weren't. In fact Felicity was so quiet always and did so little—never played games or swam—we wondered if she'd been ill and was on the cruise for her health. That was before any of us knew who they were."

"Quite. Well, they began making experiments with some of their equipment. They had a very strong, thin, flexible wire that was attached to a belt at one end and had a steel clip that locked at the other. They used it apparently for practising for high-wire work. It was invisible at a distance so it could be used if necessary before audiences, too."

"Ah," said Mrs Fairbrother, beginning to understand.

"Well, as I said, they made experiments to get the length from A deck rail to B deck rail and then, at night, when there were no passengers about, they tried putting a weight on the belt end of the wire and clipping the other end to the rail. They watched the swing of the weight as it went down in relation to the roll of the ship. They were quite scientific about it: they both understood the mechanics of their profession, Felicity especially. She's had a good deal more education than Mario, but he's no fool."

"No," said Mrs Fairbrother. "He married her, didn't he?"

Dick smiled. Shrewd old bird, he thought and continued his story.

"Their conclusion was they'd need a good roll to bring the weight right back to the ship. When it dipped their side the weight flew out and down, well clear of the side of the ship. When the roll went the other way the pull on the rail brought the weight flying back."

"I see. Ultimately Felicity was to be the weight?"

"That's right. They waited for the right kind of night, clear sky, a steady roll. We were in the Trades: there was no question the wind would change; it was nicely behind us. But they waited a bit too long. The conditions that night were more severe than they'd looked for. But we were due in at Bermuda the next day, so they had to go into action."

"I know how they managed to impress Conchita and all the rest of the play acting," Mrs Fairbrother said. "It was the disappearance we couldn't understand. Go on."

"We were briefed to stand by for the experiment. The Fenestris were cool as cucumbers. They had complete confidence in their wire and their calculations and their timing. Actually they needed a bit of luck as well. Felicity had never actually rehearsed as the weight on the wire. She relied on her skill to get feet first over the B deck rail when she swung in. If anything went wrong she could signal to Mario to pull her up again. But it needed a good view of the side of the ship coming up as she rolled. The swing was first of all out and down and then up and in."

Dick shuddered, remembering.

"I was on B deck. It was the blackest night of the whole trip. Felicity could see lights on various parts of the ship, from cabin windows and the portholes on C deck. She can't have seen very much else. But she did it. I saw her come whistling in, holding the wire in gloved hands, her toes pointed, her back arched and driving straight for the side of the ship between the two decks."

"Terrifying!"

"It certainly was! I thought she'd had it. Broken legs or spine, or a cracked skull, even if she got her legs down in time. But she did it. She can't have seen the rail till she was practically over it but she swung her feet down, letting her head drop back. She was over the rail with her back arched at an incredible angle. I was so stiff with fright I couldn't move to stop her banging down on the deck."

"Probably less hurt than if you had tried to help," Mrs Fairbrother suggested.

"You may be right. She was winded for a couple of minutes and by that time I was able to help her up. And d'you know what she said?"

"How could I? Go on."

"She said, 'The floor's wet. I slipped. You ought to have sanded it.'"

"Was that all?"

"That was all. I apologised. She grunted and gave a few tugs to the wire. The signal to Mario above. Then she wound it in, unhitched the belt and said, 'Now I must go to Captain Crowthorne.' So I took her up to the bridge. And all she said when she got there was "Jack, I'm soaking wet to the skin. Where's Ann?'"

"While Mario saw to Conchita. What a marvellous

pair they are."

"*Formidable*, as they say in France. Yes, in their own way, yes," Dick agreed. He had not enjoyed the experience.

"You said they needed luck. How?"

"The light for one thing. The sea for another."

"The sea? Why?"

"With the roll as severe as it was that night she might have been caught by a wave as she went out and down. They were fifteen to twenty feet that night, with breaking tops. I'm sure they hadn't allowed for that. If she'd been struck by a wave her whole movement would have been wrecked even if it hadn't pulled her off her wire or beaten her against the hull. You can't do much against a real sea, you know."

It was Mrs Fairbrother's turn to shudder.

"I suppose not. Yes, it must have been a terrible sea. B deck was slippery with sea water, I expect."

"It was. I couldn't have kept it dry. The spray was coming over quite often. As I said, she had the luck to do her act in the interval between the big waves."

They were both silent for a time, then Mrs Fairbrother signalled to a steward.

"I think we both need a drink after that story," she said. "What will you have?"

Salena swept up the Channel against a biting east wind, very typical of early May. There were streaks of snow on the hills above the Needles as they entered the Solent. The passengers disembarked at Southampton muffled up in all the heavy clothes in which they had left England three weeks before.

Mrs Fairbrother took leave of all her new friends, knowing they were not likely ever to meet again.

"I intend to keep in touch with Sally and Tim," she said to each couple in turn. "They will have been back for a week, but they may be able to tell me how our little drama ended."

"They lived happily ever after," said Lady Meadows

hopefully. "At least I'm sure Tim and Sally will. When they are married he won't be so—so adventurous—I trust."

"I really meant the Fennisters."

"Oh, they'll be all right," Fred Newbuckle said. "Talented, popular, they'll make their fortune. Look at the advertisement that story'll give them."

"It is the other couple we must hope for," said Mr Bernstein. "I would be uneasy for Conchita if I could find any sympathy for her, which I cannot."

Later, when they had read the English newspapers and talked to their friends, Lottie Bernstein said, "Of the Fennisters there has been news, so everyone tells us. But of that other couple, reunited, there has been nothing."

"They were not important."

"They were very important. That Ambrosan—was it—he was the most important. He was the whole reason for Conchita's. . . ." She left the complicated case of Conchita undescribed. But Max had lost interest in the case, so she made no further effort to explain.

The newspapers had indeed failed to report the end of that secondary story, because for three weeks they were not aware of it. The police on Bermuda knew that the couple had not left the island though they let it be understood that they had done so. It was not until three weeks later that they discovered what had happened.

When Ambrosan led Conchita from the wharf he took her, unresisting, silent, too spent for tears, to an empty house where he had been sheltering, having very little money, since he arrived in Bermuda from Barbados to await *Selena*'s appearance. He led Conchita in, his arm still about her, kicked the door shut behind them, dropped her bag on the floor and still embracing her, still without speaking, lifted her knife and drove it again and again into her back.

When he was sure that she was dead, Ambrosan took the knife again and cut his own throat.